Spellborn

To Karen

who I wish was here to read this dream

Prologue

Dark, brutal magic, *that* was the chaos that reigned around the kingdom of Aiden for decades. A sorcerer with great power named Koening had taken over the kingdom, leashing the royal family into his grasp. He and his followers overthrew the royal family, chambering the king and queen away. Separating them from their only daughter into the rooms of the palace that were guarded around the clock. In taking over the kingdom Koening also released any previous laws and rules that encompassed the use of the magic that Aiden thrived on.

With the sky in constant darkness and the people of Aiden weak, magic and those chosen by the gods to use it moved through the country unchecked. A large group of elves, those who believed magic users should be given free reign, backed Koening. Their love of power blinding them to the dark lord's true intention. The key to Koening's strength was the many years he spent studying magic and how it flowed through the world's core to the gifted users, the Spellborn. Magic could be harnessed by those who wielded it, pulled from an unseen source within them. Koening was obsessed with power, always looking for ways to expand his own. After years of trying to discover how to siphon more from the others, earning nothing but stacks of bodies as rewards of his work, he turned his attention to trying to figure out where it went to after it was used. His studies allowed him to find that after magic was expelled, small scraps of it were left behind, flowing into the world around it. Enriching the land, nourishing it. With his new discovery it wasn't long before Koening discovered how to pull these scraps for his own use. His strength grew and grew, seeping the leftover magic from the kingdom, killing it in the process.

Over time long established laws now shattered into chaos, the kingdom continued to descend into disorder. Koening, obsessed with honing his magic, ignored the cries from the outer territories and war broke out against the lands on the border. Magic users enslaved the people of towns to fight their battles for them. And with each battle fueled by magic, Koening pulled more power from the kingdom itself. Often times visiting the ravaged battle grounds looking for leftover magic like the ravens that poked around the bodies for scraps.

Slowly the environment began to weaken. With all spare magic being siphoned away, streams started drying up, forests, and fields of crops began dying. The effects only making once fought over lands now worthless to lords who won them.

Upset over the state of their lands, anger and betrayal fueled the lords as they sought answers and justice from their new king. They brought their cases to the palace, expecting to find a ruler and instead met a tyrant who was too engulfed in the lust of power to care of the fates of his people. These men who had hoped to find salvation for their lands instead met fates that kept them from ever seeing those same lands again.

The kingdom grew unsettled, rebel riots began breaking out. But death was all that waited for anyone who dared try interfere with the Kings syphoning of magic.

One night a great blast of power erupted from the castle, the effects of which could be felt across all of Aiden. As the last ripples of the blast flare faded, so too did magic. Suddenly all magic users lost the ability to grasp at their power. Even the smallest of spells failed them. And with the loss of power, Koening too disappeared from the world.

As the morning dawned on the now magicless kingdom of Aiden, the once thought lost Princess Collete stepped forward as Aiden's new queen.

Whispers quickly spread on how the young princess had not only freed herself from the imprisonment, but had been able to defeat the seemingly all powerful Koening.

It was told that the former king and queen had somehow sacrificed themselves to kill the dark sorcerer, saving their daughter. Though the full truth of what really happened was laid to rest with the king and queen in the royal crypt during a funeral that Collete had kept untraditionally private.

With her transition to queen, Collete lowered the status of all elves that, before the dark power, had been their equals in the land to now lower than slave as punishment for the mass majority being those who turned against her and her family. The now powerless elves retreated in small communities back to the forests and mountains where they originated and in the desolate places in the kingdom few traveled. Some storytellers around the villages said they did so to hide from their shame, but there were a few dark rumors that claim they found the soul of the dark sorcerer and pulled away from society to plot his return and find how to connect back to their power.

The war waging lords were also stripped of their titles and exiled from their now worthless lands to find work wherever they could. Many left Aiden entirely, choosing to try to remake themselves in the neighboring countries.

As the years passed by with the kingdom ruled by Collete and her bloodline, Aiden rebuilt. Crops were coaxed back from the parched earth and the dry creek beds began to trickle streams of crystal clear water once again. Little by little, the kingdom recovered. But it came at a cost that begat a secret; one that each first born princess would subsequently keep sealed within their heart and hands, a precious heirloom. Yet as the kingdom fought to heal, others plotted to regain their long lost power and glory. Those few held a secret of their own; the dark power that peaked and prodded at the edges of the kingdom, looking for a tear in the strength that it might once more, take hold.

Chapter One

Princess Arida sat in front of the looking glass in her bedchamber. Her lady's maids hands ran through her dark brown hair, moving it and shaping it into a pattern of braids around her head. She watched the small pale hands lift and wrap, lift and wrap. Her expression unchanging from her usual cold, unfeeling stare. The lady's maid pushed in the last of the pearl tipped pins before turning to the small cushion topped table sitting next to the vanity. A delicate gold tiara bejeweled with black diamonds and swirling filigree work sat glinting in the light that poured in from the window. She lifted the tiara up and placed it expertly atop Arida's head, the three-pointed arches raising artfully above the sweeping cascade of hair. Securing it with matching gold pins positioned it firmly in place.

Arida stood, her dark green dressing gown bundled tightly around her, protecting her from the cold of the stone room. Goosebumps raised the hair on her arms and she rubbed at them to warm herself. In spite of the fire in the large hearth, the autumn chill still seeped through the large walls of the bedchamber. With a straight back Arida moved across to the dressing screen, her lady a step behind her. She strolled behind the screen and pulled the ties of the robe until it slipped off her shoulders and pooled on the ground. Standing in her chemise she swiftly grabbed the red brocade gown off the sitting bench and stepped into it. Pulling it up her shoulders Arida stepped out from behind the screen and allowed the maid to assist buttoning the back of the gown. As the maids' fingers worked swiftly up Arida's back the princess reached up and fiddled with the chain around her neck. Her mind wandered back to her lesson yesterday with mother on the importance of monitoring the ocean trade routes between Aiden and Falla, their nearest neighbor. She glanced up at herself in the full-length mirror that sat against the wall.

She watched her hand gently twist around the chain, a small habit she had gotten into lately. The thick decorative rope made out of solid gold was built to support the heavy pendant discreetly nestled down the front of her gown. Its permanent resting place, safe from view. Even her closest ladies had only guessed on the design of the heirloom. Arida always bathed herself and the ladies were to never follow her behind the dressing screen, they were to wait on the other side until she came out to have the dress buttoned, or tied. And so, it had been since it was bestowed on her three years ago. Though Arida was never known for being warm and welcoming to her maids or the ladies of the court previously and that only increased since her mother looped the chain over her head on the evening of her sixteenth birthday.

Arida had been surprised when she had gone to say good night to her parents that evening and her mother had pulled the heirloom from around her neck and placed it over Arida's. Her mother explained that since turning sixteen signified a royal heir could rule the kingdom of Aiden themselves without a guardian should the need arise, it was also time for the responsibility of the amulet to be transferred. She had gazed into the stone curiously before looking up at her parents. They both wore expressions of pride tinted with a hint of worry. And to this day Arida couldn't decipher the meaning of the worry.

Ever since she was a child, Arida was always described as cool, stern and aloof by the staff that worked in the castle. Maids would whisper how odd it had been that the queen had never brought on a nurse or nanny to care for her daughter, only a few specially trained instructors when she was older. Choosing instead to have Arida with her at all times. Teaching her the ways of ruling at first by having Arida always a step behind her as she went on with her daily routine. Only placing her in the care of a Lady of the court who had a child of similar age to the princess when required to discuss choices for the kingdom that were best not heard by children's ears. But then as Arida grew older she would be seen moving through the castle as straight backed as the queen and on her way to secret meetings in the queen's private library. The staff always dismissed before any whisper of word could be eavesdropped. Even the King didn't sit in on the discussions between his wife and daughter. During these times in Arida's childhood, it was the queen who wore the secret jewelry piece. It too always tucked in to her bodice as Arida does now, only the chain visible.

Now Arida waited as her lady stooped to slide on matching dark red slippers. Her outfit now complete, she grabbed the end of her skirt and strode across the room. The chamber doors swept open on que with the echoing of her steps. Arida proceeded down the long grey stone hall, her guards who were stationed outside the door followed behind as she made her way through the castle to the throne room. Their co-ordinating dark red armor matching the kingdom's official colors clinked and echoed down the halls. The shades of red paired with the changing leaves on the sycamore tree that Arida could see out the windows that ran the length of one side of the hall.

Turning right they entered the main entry hall. Portraits of Arida's ancestors lined the walls. Previous queens stared down at them, all with the same dark brown, almost black hair that was signature to the bloodline. One small detail could also be recognized in all the queen portraits, an intricately woven decorative gold chain resting along the collar bone, dipping as if weighed down into the bodice of their gowns. The chain was a rope design that was common enough in the fashion of higher-ranking members of the court not to cause to much unwanted attention. The true intrigue was in the pendant that no one saw.

Arida paused just outside the door to the throne room. A set of guards stationed on either side reached in a synchronized motion to open the doors. Arida stepped through, her chamber guards shifted into a position lining the hallway to wait.

The inside of the throne room was grand. Large white marbled stone columns were erected to follow the natural circular shape of the room. Each had a carved solid gold eagle in various stages of flight connecting them to the domed ceiling, the birds glinted in the pale sunlight that came in from the wall of windows opposite the doors. The eagle also appeared on the family crest tapestry hanging behind the raised stone dais that sat on the far end of the room. Rich red rugs molded up the steps and led to the three large gold thrones, each furnished with gold embroidered red velvet cushions which solely occupied the dais. Two of the thrones were currently occupied. One with a large foreboding man, with red hair and a thick beard. A tall gold crown rested on top of his proud head, a perfect match to the smaller one resting on the woman's head sitting in the throne next to him. Her dark hair a perfect match to Arida's. Her parents, King Harland and Queen Varidia. Both watched Arida as she moved gracefully across the large rugs that created an aisle up to the thrones. Members of the court lined the path, all watched and bowed to her as she moved slowly to the empty throne next to her parents.

As she got closer a dark figure dressed in black and grey moved from behind her father's throne. Her mother's brother, her uncle, and the official advisor to the throne, Lord Gallis. A man small in stature, he fit well into his role as information gatherer. He was several years his sister's senior, and it showed in the grey hairs that replaced the dark ones on his head. He was usually found drifting between the ear of the queen and king, silently shifting between the backs of their thrones. His small black, hawklike eyes missed nothing in or around the court. Currently those eyes were scanning the gentlemen and ladies of the court who were milling around the outer curves of the room, all with the same bored expressions. Showing how they truly felt about being required to be present for the day's proceedings.

Arida paused at the base of the dais and dipped a small curtsy at her parents. Both offered an incline of their head in way of greeting and no more. Their icy expressions mirroring the ones they themselves had trained onto Arida's. At the signal of greeting Arida took the five steps up and seated herself on her throne. A dark shadow swept into the corner of her eye.

"Good morning, princess" Her uncle's slithering voice whispered in her ear. Arida fought the shiver that worked its way down her spine.

"Good morning uncle." She replied, fear of his face being suffocatingly close to hers kept her from turning towards him.

"You look particularly lovely this morning, the court colors become you as they do your mother."

"Thank you." Arida could swear she felt his hand running up and down the back of her throne.

Thankfully, before her uncle could say anything more, her father stood. With a wave of his hand the guards near the main entrance opened the large carved wooden doors revealing a line of people waiting to have discussions with the royal court. When the king reseated, the guards moved to the sides and allowed the people to enter the throne room one at a time.

The royal family sat still as statues throughout the whole court proceedings. Listening to the problems, complaints, and admirations from their subjects. They in turn offered advice, assistance, and thanks as needed. As the line shortened the gentlemen and ladies of the court grew restless, wandering around the outskirts of the room in small groups. Their quiet conversations echoing off the domed ceiling.

When only a few remained in line even Arida was feeling the pains of sitting to long ache through her bones, she longed to take a walk or have a conversation longer than a few words. She wondered how her parents did it. She herself had just become an active participator in the bi-weekly meeting with the township. Her parents had been doing it for decades.

Arida snuck a glance towards the king and queen. Both had maintained cool expressions but had offered small glimmers of emotion to their subjects such as a small smile towards a compliment or a frown when given a complaint or trouble. But through it all, neither showed signs of growing bored or wary.

Arida allowed her eyes to wander around the people of her court when a man stepped forward to the center of the room. He was tall, dark hair with a slightly rugged face. His attire was too nice for him to be a farmer, or shop keeper. But he wore no family crest upon his tunic as a diplomat or news bearer would have. The uniqueness intrigued Arida. The sternness of his jaw hinted that he was not here to offer praise. Maybe he was one of the lords who ruled small keeps on the outside of Aiden. A few of them still so new they yet had the time or resources to obtain finery with emblems.

"How may we be of assistance sir?" The queens voice rang out after the man did not immediately speak, a sign to Arida that maybe she too was beginning to grow restless as her mother rarely spoke first during this meeting.

"I am here on behalf of my great lord with a message for your majesty." The man spoke clearly in a gruff, calm voice.

"And who is your lord, sir?" The king asked. His eyes flicking to the left side of the Queen where Gallis stood looking at the man. He offered no hint that he knew anything about the stranger which happened rarely. Gallis prided himself on knowing every lord, lady and soon to be member of court of the not only Aiden, but the surrounding territories as well.

"My lord's name is of no importance, but his power is great and growing. He has sent me with a message." He stated again.

"Then speak your message sir so we may give a reply." The king replied, his voice rang out with an edge, clearly tired of the show the man was putting on.

He moved so fast Arida couldn't believe it. The mystery man was standing in the middle of the room one minute, and in the next he was running straight for the dais. A flash of steel shone in his hand as he aimed straight for Arida.

How he had gotten the weapon by the guards she had no idea but here he was, a small hand sword in his grasp, sprinting at a speed so great there had to be something other than pure man power assisting him. All of this was happening in the blink of an eye, and with the large ornate arm rests caging her into her seat, Arida had no choice but to sit and watch as the man barreled towards her.

He was a breath from reaching Arida's throne when a flash of red darted in-between her and her attacker. A clash of metal on metal rang out across the room, several ladies' screams echoed against the stone walls. A man was now braced between Arida and the assassin. His long red hair hung loose down his back covering a dark simple tunic. As her wits came back to her Arida recognized him as one of the several guards that would hide amongst the court in disguise, though his name she did not know. The muscles of his arms rippled under his shirt as he pushed his upheld sword against the attackers'. The blades pushing together caused the sound of shrieking steel to echo off the domed ceiling. The sound was teeth rattling, especially this close. The red-haired guard moved swiftly, bracing his weight on his front leg he whipped his other out and connected with the would-be assassin's stomach. The man went slack as the air whooshed out his lungs. When his sword arm also relaxed the guard pulled his own up and using the blunt end of the pommel, struck the dark-haired man square in the jaw. At that the attacker went com-pletely limp and fell to the floor like a sack of pota-toes.

The whole attack from beginning to end lasted only a few breaths. The other guards in the room had barely enough time to even draw their swords, let alone make it to Arida's aid. And as the red-haired guard turned around, she knew why. His ears were elongated and they pointed elegantly through his hair that was tussled from his fight, an elf.

Since the fall of the elves many who swore al-legiance to the throne took jobs in service to the crown after their powers disappeared. A few skilled warriors Arida knew worked in the royal guard but Arida rarely saw them in the palace itself, let alone this close to the family. Most of them were still so distrusted even after all this time they were put on patrol at the perimeter of the kingdom.

"Are you alright my lady?" The red-haired elf asked leaning close to her, one hand braced against the arm of her throne. Arida flinched at the closeness, her eyes straying to the man unconscious on the floor. A small trail of blood slipped through his lips.

"Your highness?" The elf asked again, concern in his eyes. He scanned her quickly, looking for signs of injury. His voice was deep but his speech was polished, unlike many other palace guards who Arida could tell from overhearing conversations didn't receive proper schooling.

"Yes, thank you. I'm well." Arida replied, her tone breathless.

"Oh, my word!" The queen exclaimed rushing from her throne to her daughters. The elf guard moved to the side to allow the queen to pull Arida up by her arms and tugged her behind the thrones, putting distance between them and the man on the floor.

"Guards!" King Harland bellowed. "I want this man taken away and questioned immediately." Turning to Galis he then spoke so only those on the dais could hear. "And I want to know who this great powerful lord of his is, and how he got into my palace with weapons in the first place." The face of the king was hard as stone and his tone unyielding.

"Yes, your majesty." Gallis said with a bow. Turning he followed the two guards who were carrying the assassin between them. His hands and feet now bound with rope.

Arida watched them go, her mother's arms still around her. It was at this time she noticed the warm feeling in the center of her chest under her gown.

"Mother." Arida murmured, turning her face up to look at the queens.

"I know I feel it." Her mother's arms tightened as if to block the warmth from everyone else in the room. Their history which was drilled into Arida since it was bestowed on her stated that the heirloom was more than just a beautiful bauble but was a remnant of the magic of the past and would grow warm in the presence of magic. But in the few years she had worn it, it had remained cool.

Arida looked up from her dress and saw the Elf's eyes on her. It was said Elves had superior hearing. Arida considered their words, and assured he couldn't understand their meaning, released some of the tension in her shoulders.

"What is your name sir?" Arida asked the elf, trying to distract herself. The queen also turned her head towards him.

"Yes sir, please tell us your name so I can thank the man who so bravely saved my daughter's life properly."

"Your majesty, my name is Faelyn of the North Forest." Faelyn took a knee as he spoke, bowing his head. His hair shifted, effectively covering his ears from view. Whether on purpose or accident Arida wasn't sure. A few murmurs rippled through the crowd of the court at the name. Even hiding his ears, his title let everyone know he was of elven blood. Arida even noticed a few ladies shuffle behind their husbands, as if scared he would turn and attack them right here in court.

"Rise Faelyn of the North Forest, and take our many thanks." The queen spoke loudly, perfectly silencing the voices around them. "If there is anything we could do for you please do not hesitate to ask it. We are in your debt."

At this the queen moved, leading Arida out of the throne room back through the door the family used to exit and avoid any loitering courtiers wanting a word. Guards moved into position around them, all on high alert for any other threat. The king followed, blocking the women from the view of the crowd. After the heavy wooden door clicked shut Queen Varidia grasped Arida's arm tightly and pulled her into a private chamber off the hallway, motioning for the guards to wait outside. Harland continued down the hall with a small band of armed men following. They turned a corner out of sight, headed in the direction of the dungeons where Arida was sure the interrogation had already begun.

Chapter Two

The air in the room her mother pulled her into was dusty and stale from misuse. Without a fire in the hearth the chill from outside made the empty room bitterly cold. Arida fought to keep her teeth from chattering.

Breathy after the surprise of being swept into the chamber she turned to see her mother standing just off from the barren hearth, her fingers worrying at her mouth.

"Mother what is it?"

"Let me see it." Her mother demanded, turning and looking at her daughter. Arida pulled at the chain without hesitation. The piece was truly a thing of ethereal beauty. The first thing your eye was drawn to was the large smooth red cabochon cut ruby in the center.

The gem was incased in a braided bezel of age patinaed gold that folded and twisted into an ornate design of intricate leaves and small golden flowers that curved around the stone. The whole piece was hot in Arida's hand, far warmer than it had been tucked in between the layers of her dress and it seemed to thrum with energy.

Surprised at the reaction the stone was having, Arida held it in her palm unable to say a word. She had never experienced anything like it. The necklace had always been a normal piece of jewelry, and now it seemed to be alive.

Varidia strode towards her daughter and also peered into her hand. Her mouth grew into a small tight line.

"I just saw it this morning and it was as it always is. What is happening to it mother?" Arida looked up from the piece.

"It is as I feared the moment, I felt the heat of it against my arm." The queen began pacing back and forth, biting her nails in the same way Arida used to until her governess swatted it out of her. She could still feel the sting on her knuckles whenever she had the nervous urge.

"What was it you feared?" Arida urged, her mother's pacing making her uneasy.

"I've had an unsettled feeling these last few weeks. A nagging that I wasn't able to place, like something out in the world had changed drastically and had been missed. I spoke to your uncle about it and he had his spy's out looking for signs of power being used." She finally paused her pacing near the small glass window in the wall, her thumb nail still pressed against her lips.

"And?" Arida urged. "What did uncle find?"

The queen turned and faced her daughter "The reports have been unsure, no one has come back and said they have found magic being used but..." She moved as if to start pacing again.

"But what?"

"A handful we sent to the northern edges of our borders and none have come back. Nor can we find any sign of them."

Both women stood staring at each other. Their features so similar with their narrow faces, defined noses and large round dark brown eyes framed with the same long dark soft falling hair. Small pieces of her father softened a few edges on Arida's face though, she also had his slightly darker complexion that liked to tan in the summer months. But from a distance she was a mirror image of her mother.

"What does this mean?" Arida whispered. "Has magic come back? Is that why the man there was able to move so fast? Do you think he's Spellborn?"

Spellborns were people who were born with the ability to access magic. Those that before her ancestor Queen Collete had put a lock on all power wielding had been celebrated for the gift of being born able to access the magic of their kingdom. And, according to her mother, had begun reappearing when she herself had been a child.

"Spellborns are dangerous." Her mother agreed. "They are unchecked and appear to have full access to the magic Collete nearly died to prevent as you just saw." Her mother shuddered slightly. "Now you see why we work so hard to irradicate any we find. Imagine if Koening were to return with this power readily available?"

Arida was shocked at the mention of the dark sorcerer. "But I thought Koening was dead?"

"Disappeared does not mean dead Arida. And the kind of darkness he had ensconced himself in is hard to defeat, especially if he is able to harness magic again through Spellborns." It was a lesson back in the early spring when Arida had learned the fate of all who were discovered to be able to access magic. And that was a carefully planned disappearance orchestrated by her uncle and his men, followed by a quick death in an attempt to keep the rumor of magic users to a minimum.

"But to answer your question, I'm not entirely sure what all of this means. Your father will fill me in on what he and Gallis' find out. If that man was truly using magic that means the dark power may being trying to come back."

"So what do we do?" Dread twisted in Arida's gut at the thought of magic coming back to the kingdom and more Spellborns arising.

The elves were the only ones alive today that remembered a world with magic in it. They had proven themselves dangerous with it then. Arida couldn't imagine them with it now.

"Well," The queen said, straightening her shoulders. "We need to work on strengthening the kingdom. Reassure the people that nothing is amiss. I'm sure word of what happened today is already spreading through the castle as we speak, nothing stays a secret in court for long." Varidia pressed her hands down her skirts, smoothing wrinkles that were not present.

"Just tell me what you would like me to do and I will do it." Arida reached up and gently squeezed her mothers' hands. The queen returned the gesture before reaching a hand up and sweeping a stray hair from Arida's face.

"Just keep the amulet a secret for now, like always. I will speak to your father and uncle as soon as they are done and then we will decide what to do from there." She watched as Arida tucked their secrete back to its hiding place.

"What will happen to the man after he is questioned?" This was the first attack on the family Arida had ever witnessed in living memory.

"Spellborn or not, he will be executed for the attempt he made on your life, and used as an example and a message to anyone who may also think about trying. And, to whoever this lord is he served." The queen's voice was cold and precise, clearly unbothered about the would-be assassin's outcome. Arida nodded her head once in acknowledgment. With that her mother put an arm around her again and together they left the small room, empty once again.

Chapter Three

The following days Arida hardly saw anyone in her family. Even her uncle who frequently ghosted through the halls was nowhere to be seen. All were hidden away in the king's private study discussing whatever information the assassin had unwillingly given. Even though Arida was grown, it was times like these that she felt like a child again. Whenever she asked if she could join the meetings her mother would just put a hand to her cheek and tell her not to worry, and when she was needed, she would be called.

So, without her daily lessons with her mother, Arida spent her suddenly vast amount of free time wandering the palace. Fall was getting into full swing and winter was slowly encroaching; fires were lit in every hearth to try to fight off the cold. Pinned between the Mathwich Mountains and the frigid Beruvian sea, the palace was always the first to experience the colder weather than the rest of Aiden. This particular morning a thick layer of frost had covered everything on the ground in the courtyard Arida was currently strolling through. She much preferred the colder weather, choosing to add extra layers to her outfits so that she could still enjoy the outside areas of the palace. Her fur lined leggings she slipped on under her gown helped keep her legs warm, her arms were covered by a short cape that buttoned near her throat.

Several of the large trees spaced around the garden were changing colors, the greens fading into yellow and dark oranges. Arida slowly walked under an arch where bright green ivy still clung to the wooden trellis, reaching up for any bit of sunlight it could find in the cloud covered sky. The white tinted grass crunched under her fur lined boots. The echoing crunch of her guards' footsteps followed her.

There were now four who followed her everywhere, double the number who usually did. Gallis's informants found no other threats currently in the palace, but since they hadn't noticed the first assassin the queen insisted on doubling Arida's guards. Luckily though, with this many guards it seemed to keep away the young eligible men of the court who always seemed to want her ear, or her arm, or whatever other piece of her they thought they could use to secure her hand in marriage.

"Good morning, my lady." A familiar voice said from Arida's right side. Turning slightly Arida saw Faelyn standing under an almost bare tree. His bright red hair stuck out among the grey, dull landscape around them.

"Good morning, Sir Faelyn." Arida replied. She paused her walk to turn and face him. She had only been able to see him briefly after the attack. Seeing him now casually leaning against the tree trunk he didn't look quite as formidable as he had mid sword battle. Though there was almost an essence that moved about him that raised the small hairs on the back of her neck, a small reminder that he was not human.

He moved away from the tree and walked towards her.

"How are you faring your majesty?" He asked stopping a few paces from her and bending at the waist in the customary bow.

"Very well, sir. Thanks to your bravery I am unscathed." Inwardly she recalled the nightmares that had plagued her since the incident, but that was something she planned on telling no one. Not even her mother for fear of her insisting on another two guards.

"Do not think of it my lady, my job is to guard you and your family. I am just glad I was so close." He straightened and Arida was able to get a clear view of him. His face had the typical handsome features of the elves, where it looked like the gods chiseled him out of rock. His skin looked sun kissed even though the castle hadn't seen the sun through the gloomy skies in weeks. He was tall, and Arida could tell well-muscled from how his tunic and sleeves contoured and tugged around his biceps. Especially when he shifted and crossed his arms behind him. Looking back at her guards Arida wondered how she never noticed Sir Faelyn before. Compared to him the other men of the guard looked positively ordinary.

"Yes, it was astonishing that you were able to reach my side before any other guard had so much as unsheathed their swords." The words were out before she could stop them. His back suddenly straightened.

"Are you insinuating your highness, that I made it to your aid using means that are forbidden in this kingdom?" His features and body language grew guarded. His shoulders tightened, straightening his back even more than it already was. The fabric of his sleeves tightening even more. Arida tried not to notice. She mentally shook herself. Of course, he would be upset by her small accusation. To be called Spellborn was to be condemned to death. Although now that Arida thought about it, she wasn't sure if the name was given to elves since before the fall it was rare for one to not have access to the magic.

"No," Arida said, looking back at her guards again who were luckily far enough behind her they seemed to not hear their conversation. "I was merely just commenting on your agility and speed. I'm sure it has to do with your elven blood."

This comment didn't seem to help his mood. His face darkened.

"Ah yes my lady, an opinion I am sure you formed from all the elves you have met." His tone was sarcastic, his words spoken with an edge.

Arida bristled "I may not have met many elves, but I have studied their history and culture. And you speak rather boldly to your princess *sir*."

"Well, I apologize your highness but I didn't know I was standing with an expert of my *culture*." Faelyn dipped into a slight bow; a smug grin pulled on his lips. He seemed to enjoy antagonizing her, a feeling Arida was not used to. Instantly she felt her face reddening in anger and embarrassment. She was just about to make a short retort when the amulet blazed hot against her chest. Arida gasped and clutched at her gown trying to pull the scorching piece far enough away from her skin to stop the burning but her lady's maid had been extra thorough in her lacing this morning and the bodice of her gown clung to her like a second skin.

"My lady?" Faelyn said alarmed by Arida's sudden strange reaction. He closed the distance between them looking at her chest where her hands clawed at the material. All signs of irritation faded from his features. Arida suddenly recalled the reason as to why the pendant had grown hot the last time and wildly looked around the courtyard.

"What is it? What are you looking for? Are you alright?" Faelyn asked quickly following her gaze. Arida's guards seeing the scene before them started moving towards the pair. Just as the guards made their first steps towards them an arrow soared through the air seemingly out of nowhere, and punched through the chest armor of the lead guard. A look of surprise froze on his face before he stumbled and fell to the ground.

"Take cover!" The second closest guard yelled out as the remaining two next to him drew their swords and looked in the area that the arrow appeared.

Not waiting for permission Faelyn grabbed Arida around the waist and pulled her close to him, tucking her near his chest. Arida hadn't realized just how tall Faelyn was, but now pressed against his chest she noted the top of her head tucked just under the elf's chin. His arms, just as muscled as she had thought, wrapped around her as he moved, careful not to get his legs tangled in her voluminous skirts. He rushed them as fast as he could to the nearest door. Another arrow flew right by Arida's head, missing her by an inch before lodging into the tree next to them. The amulet flared hot again pulling a shocked gasp from her mouth as a third arrow flew towards them. Faelyn threw his weight forward, dragging both of them to the ground, his body covering hers.

"Are you alright?" he gasped as his eyes raked over her, looking for any signs of injuries. Arida nodded her head to let him know she was uninjured.

Out of the corner of her eye another guard fell from an arrow to his throat. With the elf's body so close to hers she had no doubt he could feel the flash of heat that flared from the hidden jewel. Arida shrieked and continued clawing at her chest. She finally grabbed a hold of the thick gold chain hanging from her neck and pulled.

Faelyn's face was one of shock when the large pendant dangled between them. The red stone once again seemed alive as a white mist swirled inside. The elves' eyes locked onto the necklace and then slowly slid to Arida's.

"What is that?" He asked as he shifted his gaze back to the stone, steam now radiated off it from the touch of the cold air around them.

Arida's eyes moved from the pendant to Faelyn. Realization that she had shown him, an outsider of the family and an elf the secret her ancestors had kept for generations burned through her.

"You are to tell no one of what you saw. Do you understand?" Her tone was cold but flustered. Faelyn just looked her in the eyes before nodding once. Voices rang out around them as more guards rushed into the courtyard. The flying arrows had seemed to stop. Slowly the pendant cooled down to its previous warm temperature, whatever magic that had been being used must have been released. Closing her hand around the stone Arida gently fed the chain down her bodice hiding it once more.

"Princess!" A cold slithering voice yelled out. "Princess Arida!"

"Over here, uncle." Arida yelled back. Slowly Faelyn stood, pulling Arida up with him. His body still shielding her from the courtyard. When no arrows immediately flew at them, he led her back to the center of the garden. They passed the bodies of Arida's guards, small pools of blood gathered around them. Their still open eyes already had a glaze over them. Arida moved closer to Faelyn, careful not to step in any of the blood.

They moved around one of the trees and Gallis came into view. He had a small group of guards all wearing the black color of his personal spies around him, all on alert with swords drawn. Gallis looked at the pair as they approached, his eyes scanning them up and down.

"Arida." He seemed to hiss the words. "Thank goodness you're alright."

Arida stopped a few paces from her uncle. The elf also stopping one step further, placing himself slightly between her and the blacked garbed men.

"Yes uncle, unfortunately I can't say the same for my guards. Have your men found who fired at us?" Arida noted the lack of stray arrows littering the ground. It appeared all but the ones that had barely missed her had found their mark.

"No, they have eluded us. Did you see where they were shooting from? By the time I arrived the arrows had stopped." He stared at the arrow poking out of the first guard's chest. No emotion showed on his face. "The angle of this arrow looks like it came from the southern wall." He crouched closer to the body, the edge of his cloak trailed through the puddle of blood surrounding it. Arida wondered if this was why he and his guards wore all black, to hide the blood. "I don't suppose you saw how many shooters there were?" Gallis asked, still not looking up from the arrow protruding from the guard's chest.

"No, I didn't, after the first arrow landed, we turned and fled near the door on the other side of the court-yard. I was too busy trying to get there I didn't look at where the arrows were coming from." Arida replied.

Gallis's eyes flicked up finally to Arida's face and then moved to Faelyn who was still standing very close to her side.

"And what about you, elf? It appears that yet again you seemed to be in the right place at the right time. How lucky for us." He crooned while rising back to his full height which like Arida, was a head shorter than the elf.

Faelyn's back went rigid at the elf comment and the hidden implication before replying "Yes, we all must be lucky. I am once again just glad I was here to help her highness. But like her, no I did not see the shooters. The arrows did come from the southern wall, but my main focus was to cover the princess and get her to safety."

As he spoke Arida held her breath hoping he would do as she asked and tell no one that he had seen the amulet. As Faelyn finished speaking and looked back at her uncle, she let out a small sigh of relief. She noticed Faelyn's eyes flick quickly in her direction and then go back to her uncle. Who hadn't seemed to notice.

"What a shame." Gallis said "It seems to me you should have been able to focus not only on keeping your princess safe, but also on where the threat was coming from so you could report as much information as possible about the attack to your superiors. Or were you not trained for such things? Perhaps I need to have a meeting with the General and offer my advice on rectifying this problem." The corners of Gallis's mouth twitched up into a small snarl. As not only an advisor to the throne, but the queen's brother, Gallis always liked to remind people of his rank. Especially those he viewed as lesser beings.

"Yes, sir I was, but in the midst of the attack my sole focus was on seeing the princess to safety. As her uncle I am sure you will agree that is always my top priority, and as your own private guard can attest, I was trained to protect the royal family above all else." Faelyn gave a cursory glance over to the six guards all adorned in the black color of Gallis's private police.

Gallis visibly bristled and opened his mouth to make a retort when a stern female voice spoke over him.

"Gallis, you forget your manners." The queen strode from behind him and moved in-between the men. "Here Sir Faelyn has saved our Arida yet again and you choose to question him as if it was, he who shot arrows across our courtyard, and not who kept her alive." Gallis dropped his head at the sharp tone of his sister. Turning from him, Varidia looked at Faelyn.

"Once again, I owe you a debt of gratitude for saving my daughter. Though appreciated I truly hope this is not going to become a habit."

Faelyn bowed to the queen. "Your majesty it is always my honor to keep you and your family safe. I am also once again just glad I could be here to be of service. And I am greatly sorry for the men you have lost today."

"Thank you, they were indeed great men and I will make sure that their families know they died saving the life of their princess." The queen glanced towards the bodies lying around them, a tinge of sorrow flashed across her face before the mask came back. "Arida I would like you to go to your chamber and wait for me. There are some things I would like to discuss with you privately but I need to finish things up down here first."

"Of course, mother." Arida whispered making to move back inside.

"Sir Faelyn, if it's not too much to ask would you kindly see Arida to her chamber and stand guard outside until I arrive. I will bring replacements for her personal guard with me so that you can return to your duties."

"Of course, your majesty, it would be an honor and a privilege." Faelyn bowed again before turning and followed Arida as she walked back into the castle. Her mother's echoing voice ordering Gallis's guards to carefully remove the fallen men from the courtyard followed them until they reached the main hallway. Faelyn was silent and only stopped following once she reached the door to her bed chamber.

"I will be out here if you need anything." He turned and stood with his back near the wall, the picture of a member of the royal family's private guard. The only difference being his attire, he was dressed as he had been the other day in clothes that let him blend in to the people around him and not stand out as a member of the palace guard. Without another word Arida disappeared into her bed chamber to await her mother.

Chapter Four

Arida paced her bedchamber back and forth for several hours waiting for her mother to show up. After her feet grew sore, she sat on the edge of her four-poster bed and watched the flames dance inside her fireplace. As the light outside began to dim Arida heard voices outside the door. One was distinctly female.

After a few moments the door quietly opened and the queen stepped through. Arida rushed to her mother's open arms. They stood there for a moment, just holding each other. The feelings of today finally able to be released.

"When I heard what had happened, I thought my heart stopped. I got there as soon as I could." Varidia whispered into her daughter's hair.

"Why does this keep happening? Who wants me dead so badly that they would try twice in the same week?" Arida asked pulling back enough to see her mother's face.

"I'm not sure dear, I wish I did but I just don't know." Slowly they walked arm and arm to the sitting chairs set up by the hearth. "Your father, uncle and I have been in conversations all week as you know. We have been trying to figure out exactly who could have hired the assassin. The man gave us very little before he died and never divulged a name. We have also been sending correspondence to the neighboring kingdoms to ask if they will send aid if the need arises. We have yet to hear back but that is not all too surprising. We are after all asking for help against a threat that we only know calls himself a powerful lord. I know I would be skeptical responding if I received such a letter."

A log popped in the hearth sending small sparks across the plush cream rug that lay on the floor in front of their feet. One caused a small singe mark on the edge. Arida looked at it without feeling.

"I had a conversation with the guard Faelyn before I came in." Her mother looked up from the rug and met Arida's eyes. "He has offered to fill the space of one of your guards we lost today." Arida shifted in her seat with surprise. "And I have every intention of taking him up on that even if your uncle seems dead set on him being involved with this somehow."

"And why are you so sure he isn't?" Arida asked before she could stop herself. The thought of Faelyn being involved had not crossed her mind during each of the attempts on her life. But she could see why her uncle was so skeptical on the convenience of the elf's timing. Though she loathed to agree with that man.

"For one thing it would have been far easier to allow the attacks to happen if he was working with the person trying to kill you. Plus, he may have known you would be in the throne room but he had no way of knowing you would be in the courtyard this morning."

"What if his plan was not to kill me those two times, what if it was to gain our favor and trust." Arida shifted again uncomfortable with talking about him like this with him standing just outside the door. She knew elves had exceptional hearing but could they hear through stone walls?

"Maybe it is." The queen replied. "But if that is true then him getting closer to us means we are closer to him too. His every move will be being watched by you, me, your father and, gods know, your uncle."

Arida processed the information her mother had laid out in front of her.

"So, what do we do now?"

"Now, we wait. We wait to hear back from the neighboring kingdoms and we wait to hear if we find anything from the attack today. Until then I expect you to go nowhere without your new guard, and please refrain from wandering out of doors until we put an end to all of this."

Arida wanted nothing more than to object to her mother adding even more restrictions on her but she knew better than to try. All it would do is cause a fight and the people she had to talk to was already small enough. "The amulet grew hotter today than the time before, it nearly burned me." Was all Arida could say in reply. She had even checked her skin for a burn when she had returned to her room, but it hadn't so much as turned red.

"Did anyone see it?" Her mother asked. Arida knew what she really meant, had Faelyn seen it.

"No" Arida lied. "I kept it safe.

"Good".

Arida's mother left a few moments after their conversation to meet with her father. Whether or not her mother heard the lie on her lips Arida wasn't sure. Her stomach began to growl and her fire was growing small so she called for her lady's maid to attend to her needs. In the split seconds her door was open Arida peered out and saw Faelyn standing like a statue in the same position he was in when she had left him. He didn't so much as glance her way.

After finishing her dinner tray Arida allowed her maid to assist her in unlacing her gown before dismissing her for the night. Once in her nightgown Arida slipped between the sheets and settled down.

Slowly she slipped off to sleep and fell into a long night filled with nightmares each ending with her and her family's death at the hands of an unknown dark figure.

Chapter Five

When Arida shot up in bed hours later her legs were entangled in the sheets causing a brief moment of panic that the nightmare had been real and she was in fact trapped. After she swept her sweat soaked hair out of her face, she was able to see she was in her own room, alone. Her shoulders sagged in relief. Taking a deep breath Arida disentangled herself from her bed and padded on bare feet to the washroom. After washing the sweat from her brow, she grabbed her dressing gown and a pair of slippers before sitting in front of the darkening hearth, watching the burning embers flicker. The coolness of the room calmed her heated skin.

After only a few minutes Arida was up again pacing around her room. It was at this moment her window caught her eye, at the darkness that flooded in. Morning was still hours away; her lady's maid would not be up until sunrise. But suddenly the bedchamber was too small. The air still seemed too hot to her sweat dampened skin. She had to get out. Hopeful that her guards had stepped away Arida creaked open the door to her room. A flash of red hair instantly greeted her.

"Princess, is something the matter?" Faelyn asked turning towards the crack in the door. At first glance you would think he had stayed in the same position all night. But upon further inspection his tunic had been changed to one of deep red for the royal guard. His hair which had no adornment earlier now had a small braid hanging on either right side of his face, keeping hair from falling forward.

"Uh, no nothing at all. I just thought I would take a walk." Arida pulled the top of her robe a little closer.

"A walk?" Faelyn asked glancing at the darkness out the window at the end of the hall and back at her with a raised brow.

"Yes." Arida replied indignantly "A walk."

"Well then." Faelyn replied with a half-smile "After you." He gestured down the hall with one hand, the other resting easily on the pommel of his sword.

Drawing up to her full height Arida stepped forward out the door and started walking down the hall towards no particular destination. After a few random turns she realized from the increased heat and faint scent of bread in the air that they were getting close to the castle kitchens. Making as if she was planning to go there all along Arida strode towards the solid oak doors leading into the large room.

The air that washed over her was incredibly warm, almost sweltering. A long wooden work table cut the room in half; the ovens were glowing softly against the far wall. A man in a chef's hat and apron was dozing peacefully in the corner. Unsure of what to do next Arida stood like a statue in the doorway. The kitchens were one place she had never been to before. Faelyn walked in behind and looked at her questioningly. "Was there something you needed in here princess?" He asked in a whispered voice.

"Um not particularly, and please just call me Arida." She whispered back. She had never asked any other guard to call her by her name. And she wasn't entirely sure why she was letting the elf. Although she had never really had much conversation with any other guard she'd had. They were usually just silent figures that stayed nearby.

"Ok Arida. Are you hungry at all? I could get you something." He gestured towards the cabinets on the right-hand side of the room.

"Oh, no I'm okay. Thank you." Shifting to wrap her arms around herself Arida suddenly felt very uncomfortable in the kitchen.

"Well," Faelyn started seeing the shift in her stance "I can escort you back to your bedchamber unless there was some other spot you wanted to wander aimlessly too and stand in." Turning to face him she could see the ever-present smirk resting on his face.

"I wasn't wandering aimlessly; I knew exactly where I was going."

"Oh, is that so? Then pray tell what was the grand purpose of coming to the kitchens if you were not hungry and needed nothing from here. Unless of course you just wanted to spy on the baker napping by the ovens?"

Arida opened her mouth, couldn't think of a retort and closed it again. After a moment and still nothing to say came to mind she turned on her heels and stalked out of the kitchen with a huff. A soft chuckle followed her along with the soft thud of the door closing. Going off memory Arida back tracked to her room, or where she thought her room was. She had been raised in this castle her whole life, but she rarely went anywhere without being guided by one of her maids, guards or the occasional page. And never at night. She was surprised how differently the stone halls looked in the dark. After rounding the final turn, she expected to see the door to her bedchamber. Instead, she came to the entrance of one of the stair-cases that led to the study towers where the libraries and offices for the higher-ranking lords were.

"Wanting to go up and not get a book like we went to the kitchen to not eat?" A smug voice asked from behind her.

Arida's back stiffened as her mind reeled for a possible reason she'd have to come to one of the studies. Before she could make a response, quick footsteps echoed through the hall. The sound growing louder as the steps grew closer. Arida swiveled her head from left to right looking for a place to hide. If her mother learned of this little adventure, she'd for sure restrict Arida to the confines of her room.

"Quick, back here." Faelyn's voice whispered. Turning, Arida saw him sweep a tapestry back revealing a small nook hidden behind it.

"How did you...?" Arida began before being hushed and gestured at to move quickly behind the makeshift curtain. Quickly and with soft slippered feet Arida tucked into the small alcove. Faelyn followed and allowed the tapestry to fall back, effectively hiding both of them. The space was small and Faelyn's back pressed against her, pushing her into the cool stone. The echoing grew closer and closer, and then the sound of a second set of footsteps joined them. These new steps had a steady rhythmic sound, someone was coming down the study stairs. The set in the hall slowed and stopped from the sounds of it just in front of the tapestry with the secret hiding spot.

Arida held her breath, and from what she could feel, Faelyn wasn't breathing either.

"You've been sloppy." A male voice hissed in whispers, the tone of the voice sounded familiar to Arida, but without being able to see through the thick woven material that was also blocking them from view she just couldn't place it.

"Sloppy! And how so?" A deep male voice echoed back. This one Arida didn't recognize at all.

"What do you mean how so? Bold attempts, leaving bodies. I paid you to cause fear and unrest between the family and the people, not cause scenes that they can rally behind. Going after the princess was stupid and reckless."

"You paid me to do what I do best, it's not my fault you decided to get all *soft*."

"Soft? Is that what you call it? I call it intelligence. I have worked too hard for too long to get everything lined up and create the perfect scenario for me to get into a seat of power. And I have done so *quietly*...." The familiar voice said through what sounded like clenched teeth.

Faelyn's whole body was a rock of tension as he shifted to sweep the tapestry away with one hand as his other grasped the pommel of the sword strapped to his hip. Arida quickly reached for his shoulder to still him. Yes, the conversation the two men were having was enough to charge them with high treason. For one thing the unrecognized man was the one responsible for the attempts on her life and the death of her guards. The other, who's voice Arida was racking her head to place seemed to be the one who hired him. Though it appeared he didn't condone the actions of the first, he still planned to disrupt the kingdom and from the sounds of it take the throne. And though Arida believed Faelyn could take the two men on his own, fear took over and she couldn't risk starting a fight in the hall without any back up, or witnesses to what was transpiring.

Faelyn stilled, the tapestry didn't so much as shift.

"Are you asking me to stop what you hired me for? I didn't know you would be so opposed to my methods." The man hissed in a challenging tone. "Though, if you are stopping me I will be keeping the money you so generously paid up front."

"No, I am not asking you to stop, just try not to kill anyone else... especially the princess. I have plans for her."

A shiver ran down Arida's spine at that, and she squeezed Faelyn's shoulder with the hand she had yet to move from earlier.

"Now, make yourself scarce." The familiar voice said. "We've been here to long already."

Footsteps echoed again, going opposite ways down the hall from the sound of it.

Faelyn still didn't move even after the sounds of the men's departure fell silent. Unsure what to do, Arida stayed quiet, just in case his elven ears were still picking up noises she couldn't detect.

Finally, after what felt like hours, Faelyn reached up and slowly pulled the thick fabric of the tapestry back. Arida flinched from the soft glow of the torches after being in their dark hiding spot for so long. Faelyn guided Arida back into the now empty hall as her eyes adjusted. They stood there for a few more moments just staring at each other.

"I'm not sure what to do with the information we just heard." Arida said, breaking the silence. Even her whisper felt too loud.

"Neither do I." Faelyn replied, glancing back and forth down the long hall. "My duty requires me to report what I heard, but as I am not sure who it was that was speaking, I fear not being believed or telling our story to the exact person we were listening too."

"Yes, it does appear that whoever it was out here in the hall is close to my family. And felt secure enough to meet his chaos causer here in the castle. I know the ones voice from somewhere, I just can't place it and is driving me mad."

"I was thinking the same, the one voice was oddly familiar. But garbled, almost like he was trying to mask it in case he was overheard." Faelyn rubbed at his jaw, an obvious sign of frustration. "Well, it does us no good standing here in the hall wondering. If you are done with your midnight wander, I would be happy to escort you back to your room."

Arida looked up at him, no sign of the joking humor was on his face now. Just the look of a royal guard doing his sworn duty.

"Yes, I am ready to go back to my room." Arida waved her hand towards the left as a sign for him to lead the way. And with that he began walking, to the right.

Chapter Six

The large wooden door of Arida's bedchamber clicked back into place after Faelyn exited. He had insisted on searching the room before allowing her to enter alone, since she had refused his request on getting a lady's maid to stay the night with her in her room. She claimed it was too late an hour to disturb anyone now, and by the time one was dressed and present it would be nearly dawn. Though Arida wouldn't have allowed it even if it wasn't so late. She was too exhausted to have someone fuss about the room nor did she feel right asking one of the ladies to give up sleep in their beds to take up post in a chair when she had a guard already stationed in front of the door. Plus, the idea of having someone watch her in her sleep was unsettling.

Now alone Arida wrapped her arms around herself though there was no chill. Slowly she moved her way around the large four poster bed. Arida grabbed the curtains of the large window across from the bed and pulled it open revealing the dark night. Storm clouds filled the sky hiding any stars that might have been out. Looking across she could see the lights of the closest village Clarea reflecting into the sky. Turning she approached the side of the bed and pulled the sheets back and climbed in to lay down. Laying with her face to the window Arida tried to let sleep take her, but her mind was still turning too fast.

Who was the person that belonged to that too familiar voice? And who was the man for hire that was responsible for the horrors she had witnessed? The men that were taking it upon themselves to try to hurt her, her family, and her kingdom.

Could this threat also have something to do with the amulet acting up after all these years? Was this a sign of the darkness from her kingdom's history returning. To Arida's knowledge there were not many magical objects left in the world, this amulet being one. So information about how they worked and what they were capable of now that magic was inaccessible was limited. There was one other item she knew that was locked away somewhere in the palace for safe keeping, but according to her mother it was just a shell of what it had been. That item had also gone inactive as soon as magic was gone. Laying secured away now just in case the time came magic became usable again. What it looked like and what it used to be capable of doing her mother had never shared with her. But with so few items there were far fewer people who knew how they worked. Her mother had taught her many things about the history of the necklace and how her ancestor Collete had wielded it against Koening. But how exactly she did so had been lost to time years ago. Or, perhaps never shared in the first place.

Slowly the night faded outside the window, the sky turning from dark black, to grey, to the paleness of autumn daylight. The storm clouds from the night held at bay for another day. Arida shifted up, her shoulders and back stiff from laying for so long in the same position. While rotating her neck back and forth to hopefully release some of the tension a small knock sounded on her chamber door.

"Enter." Arida spoke loud enough for her voice to carry through the thick wood and stone of the room.

"Good morning your highness." One of her lady's maids, a young new girl whose name Arida hadn't learned yet, poked her head through the now cracked door.

"Please heat up the bath water and then you may go." Arida stayed in her seated position in her bed as the woman scuttled past her into the adjoining bathing chamber. Soon the small woman came back in carrying a large bucket filled with water and placed it on a hook near the hearth. She stoked the flames to grow them from their long night of burning and added a few more pieces of wood to it from the pile nearby. The maid worked swiftly, filling the buckets, heating the water and then pouring it into the bathing tub. Soon she came back out and bowed before dismissing herself back out through the main door.

Slowly Arida removed herself from the pile of warm white sheets and walked into the bathing room. The large marble bathing tub filled the room with steam that caressed the warm flame flickering in the torches lighting up the room. Pulling the nightgown over her head Arida moved closer to the tub, dropping the garment on the floor for a servant to fold and place back on her bed later. With nothing on but the amulet Arida placed a hesitant toe into the water to test the temperature. The water was hot but not enough to scald her skin. Gently she lowered herself into the bath, sighing in relief as the heat seeped from the water and relaxed her stiff muscles.

Letting her gaze float around the room Arida took in the small portal in the wall for the well access. The bucket was placed in its designated place on the floor near the wall, but the chain that normally was rolled up onto its wheel near the top of the well was unwound hanging down. For a moment Arida assumed that the maid, being new, had merely forgot to bring the chain up after her last bucket pull, but then Arida thought the chain would still be up. The wheel that holds the chain had been designed to keep it from accidentally going down on its own, even if it had weight hanging on it. This was a convenience to keep the water bucket from falling down the long shaft if a maid grew tired. But it was firstly insisted on by the queen after a young Arida grew too curious of how far down the well actually went one morning when she was supposed to be napping. It had only been her mother's exceptional timing after an ill feeling forced her to check on her small daughter that had kept Arida from riding the hook and chain down into a watery grave. After that, a pressure plate was added to the wheel that only when pressed would allow the chain and bucket to go down the well.

Arida studied the chain, unsure of why the maid would have gone through the work of rolling the chain all the way down without the bucket and then had left it. Just then the chain seemed to shift slightly. Arida blinked several times trying to figure out if her eyes were deceiving her with the steam and small distance between her and the well. Just then it rattled again, hitting the stone on the back end of the well. Arida launched to her feet, causing water to slosh over the sides of the tub. With the sound of the water hitting the marble floor the chain shook even harder, as if whatever was on the other end of it was climbing faster. Moving quickly Arida tried to get out of the tub and reach for her dressing gown that was hanging from a small hook near the door. But with all the water that had displaced from the tub the marbled ground was slick and as soon as her first foot hit the puddle it slipped out from underneath her and she went crashing to the ground. Arida let out a cry of pain as her right side crashed against the stone. Her head followed with a resounding crack causing her vision to go momentarily black. The chain rattled again.

"Arida!" A male voice yelled from out in her room. "Is everything alright?"

Still disoriented, Arida tried to shout out to the voice for help but the air had been knocked from her lungs so all she managed was a small groan. But it must have been loud enough because the sound of boots running across her room vibrated through the floor. The blurry outline of Faelyn appeared in the doorway.

"Oh shit! Arida what happened?" Looking around quickly Faelyn grabbed the discarded night gown on the floor and draped it over Arida's naked body, kneeling by her side trying to keep his eyes away from the parts of her that were still uncovered.

"The... well..." Arida was able to gasp out as her lungs fought to get air back in them from the shock of her fall. Faelyn whipped his head to the portal in the wall, the chain now motionless. Faelyn stood and simultaneously walked forward and pulled his sword out of its sheath. A loud splash echoed up from deep in its dark tunnel. Faelyn swore under his breath, he leaned through the well cut out and tried to make anything out of the deep darkness. When it was clear the hole was too far and too dark to see down, he quickly made his way back to his fallen princess. The initial shock from the fall was wearing off and her joints and muscles were now starting to ache. But at least she felt like she could breath again.

"Hold on one moment." He said before moving swiftly out into the main bedroom. There was a rustling noise and when he returned, he had the large top sheet from her bed. Using it to completely cover Arida's body he tucked it around her as he pulled her gracefully up into his arms and carried her back to her bed.

Arida's head pounded from the movement and the bedchamber whirled around her. Setting her down gently he began carefully pulling her right arm out from the covering he had her in. Straightening it out made her wince, but he seemed to believe, as she did, that it was not broken. His fingers gently probed the side of head, a large lump had already begun growing. Arida attempted to sit up, Faelyn seeing what she was trying to do, assisted her with one hand still supporting her head, the other bracing her bare back.

As she sat up her vision whirled slightly around the edges. Arida blinked to clear it and glanced over to Faelyn. With her face so close to his she was able to study the details of the elf's face. This close she noticed he had small light-colored freckles that peppered the bridge of his nose, which with his elven blood was surprising, those type of blemishes never appeared on perfect elven skin. His eyes were a stunning green with small gold flecks in them. He seemed to notice her studying and his eyes shifted from the side of her head to lock his gaze with hers. The cocky side grin she was slowly getting used to slowly spread across his mouth.

"See anything you like, your majesty?" He slowly slid his hand away from her back. The skin tingled in its absence.

Arida cleared her throat "I'm not sure what you're talking about, I don't know where you expected me to look with you so close to my face."Faelyn leaned back chuckling. "Well, nothing seems to be broken, you have one hell of a bump on your head but it's not bleeding."

"Well thank you for, getting me off the floor."

"Oh, trust me, it was my pleasure." His grin grew even wider. Though there was still a small spark of fear lingering in those green eyes.

"You are awfully bold to speak to your princess like that." Arida grabbed the blanket a little tighter, fully remembering that she was completely naked underneath. She felt her cheeks flush.

"I'm not sure what you mean your majesty, I am just glad I could be of service to your ladyship in your time of need."

His brazen remarks had dispelled the last bit of daze from her mind. Arida almost wondered if that had been his intention all along.

"Speaking of my time of need, what do we do now that whoever is behind these attacks has figured out a way to get into my private chambers? And if you even suggest guarding me from in here I will have you banished to guard a ship out in the Beruvian sea for the rest of your days."

At this Faelyn's face grew somber.

"I am not sure; I think it would be for the best if we keep this attack a secret. And we act as if nothing has happened."

"And why do you think we should do that; my family may be able to move me into a more protective area. They could make sure they keep a closer eye on the water ways and other areas that we hadn't thought of yet."

"That's my point. At least I know this room and these halls, if we move you to a different part of the castle there may be hiding areas, secret doors that I am not aware of. I didn't know the canal access to your well was unsecure. I do now and I will have something fixed in the tunnel that will fit a bucket and nothing else. And since both of us agree that at least one of the men involved is a major player here in the castle we can't risk them knowing we are aware that these attempts are all connected." Faelyn paused looking around. "I will make a point to my commander that the staff all be double checked. I doubt the maid earlier will be back, but that doesn't mean she is the only one that has been turned, or brought in by this person."

Arida nodded her head slowly and was just about to open her mouth and ask another question when someone began banging on the bedroom door. Arida slow-ly reached for her head, the deep pounding on the wood echoed in the pulsing best in her brain. Quickly Faelyn stood from the edge of the bed, moved across the room and cracked the door open, his stance ready for anything that might try to get past him.

"What is it?" Faelyn asked not moving an inch out of the way.

"I have an urgent message for the princess." A male voice answered, the sound of armor rattled.

"Let him in." Arida responded, ignoring the look Faelyn gave her. She rubbed gently at her tem-ples trying to dispel the headache that was growing stronger.

A palace guard walked in, his face flush from run-ning. He stopped in front of Arida, his glance be-tween her still wrapped in the sheet and Faelyn was not missed by either.

"Your highness," the guard bowed "I have urgent news from her Royal Majesty."

"Go ahead." Arida replied, the stony face of the princess the rest of the world saw back on her face. Regardless of her attire.

"There was another attack this morning, I'm afraid the king was injured during it and the queen is currently by his side and requests for you to join her in their private chambers."

Arida felt for the second time this morning all the breath rush out of her body. Her gaze slid from the guard in front of her to Faelyn standing off to the side. He must have sensed her loss of words and her look as a silent plea for him to answer for her.

"Give her highness a few moments to get herself decent and then I will escort her to the queen's chambers myself."

The guard bowed and left them once again alone.

"I will give you a moment to change, and then I will bring you to the queen." Faelyn repeated before following the other guard out into the hall.

Slowly Arida moved off the edge of the bed and stood. The sheet slipped off her as she made her way to the wardrobe and went through the motions of dressing, unaware of what she was actually doing. She grabbed a gown that had buttons on the front. Her fingers moved swiftly sliding each button into place. It hung off her oddly without the layers of underclothes she normally wore but there was no time to call for a dressing maid, nor did she fully trust any of her ladies after what happened earlier. Finishing with her silk slippers Arida walked through the door and started down the hall, not looking to see who stood guard or followed. Faelyn took the lead after they made it out of her hallway. Though she needed no guidance to find the way, she appreciated the gesture. They moved through the corridors in silence, quickly passing very few others on their way to the king and queens suite.

They reached the large double doors with black iron work forming the large eagle in flight that was mirrored in the stitching on the surcoat on the guards standing on either side. Faelyn did a slight nod towards one of the men, at this signal the guard relaxed his stance and moved to open the door for the princess.

Arida moved quickly through the familiar rooms of her parents' chambers. Passing the entryway, dining room and private library she stood at the open door to the king and queen's bedchamber. The candles were dim, and the curtains were drawn closed allowing the majority of the room to be lit by the fire in the large hearth across the room from the bed. Shadows danced along the tall stone walls, causing the figures in the many tapestries decorating the walls to appear like they were moving within their scenes. Following the dancing tapestries Arida's eyes landed on the large four poster bed to the far side of the room. The soft mesh privacy curtains were drawn on all sides except for the right where her mother sat on a high back upholstered chair.

She was half leaning out of it, grasping the large pale hand of her father. The white sheets were pulled up to his chest, and tucked tightly around him. He lay so completely still that for a split second Arida thought she was already too late. Her mother lifted her gaze from the kings' hands to stare at her daughter. Her face was grave, the fire light highlighted the stains from tears on her cheeks. Arida moved slowly, her gaze flicking between the faces of her mother and father. As she stepped closer, she could see the small rise and fall of the king Harland's chest. The sound of his shallow breaths mixed with the crackling of the fire.

"What happened?" Arida said in a tone just above a whisper.

Her mother turned to look back at her husband "I went for my morning stroll with a few of the ladies from court, I was to meet your father for breakfast back here when I was done. I took longer than normal after Lady Tumane slipped on a loose stepping stone and went for a tumble. I waited with her until a healer could come and help her to one of their examining rooms. It didn't seem enough of a delay to send word to your father so I just came up after Lady Tumane was settled." Her mother paused as the King took a long-ragged breath. Both ladies tensed until his breathing retuned back into what it had been.

"When we got to the main doors to enter our chambers the guards were no longer stationed outside. I was worried and ran in and saw your father was in the dining room face down in the platter of salmon convulsing. Luckily, I still had two members of my private security with me so we were able to get him up." Her mother paused again, squeezing her eyes against more tears threatening to fall at the memory of what she had seen. "It seemed as if he was choking but there was nothing in his airway. I sent one of my men to fetch a healer as fast as he could. We got your father laying down and when the healers arrived, they started saying things about poisons and the food. They shoved countless tonics down his throat until the choking sounds stopped and he finally relaxed. After we got him into bed the healers cleared the food off the table to test. He's been like this ever since." Her mother finished her story in a low whisper, brushing her free hand across her husband's forehead. Arida stood there absorbing all that had been said. Her mind reeling at the thought that if Lady Tumane hadn't stumbled, her mother would have been here on time to start their morning meal together and gods know if they would have been found in time.

"Is he going to make it?" Arida asked putting her hand on her mother's shoulder.

"They aren't sure, we aren't sure how long he was without breath before I got here. They worry that could have affected him more than the poison."

The women watched quietly as the man they both loved lay in the bed struggling to breathe.

"Has he awakened at all since the tonic was given to him? And where were his guards?" Arida asked breaking the silence.

"I haven't the slightest idea where the guards went. Gallis is trying to find that out now. And no, he has not woken yet." Her mother replied "And I truly fear he never will." At this the queen's shoulders slumped Arida realized how much her mother really loved her father. Arida always knew her parents were affectionate to each other. Unlike many of the other kingdoms that visited, her parents shared a bedchamber, they danced together at every ball and more than the obligatory first dance that started the festivities. But sitting here, watching her mother's sorrow radiate off of her, she for the first time could see the full extent of her love.

Unable to look anymore at her father in the bed or her mother in the chair, Arida let her gaze shift back around the room. Faelyn was standing in the library just outside of the doorway of the bedchamber. His gaze met hers and she could see the pity there. She looked away again and gave her mother's shoulder a slight squeeze.

Chapter Seven

Arida stood next to her mother until a servant who came in to tend to the fire snagged another chair and set it next to the queens. Arida tended to her mother as she tended to her husband. When she dribbled broth down his throat Arida also coaxed a few small bites of meat and cheese into her mother, after the newly appointed royal tasters sampled some bites first. Every time Arida glanced back, Faelyn was in the same spot, unmoving.

Eventually Arida's body grew so stiff it began cramping muscles in her back, legs and neck. Her head was again pounding with a dull headache. Reminders that there were two attacks today. But she had done as Faelyn asked and not shared that event with her mother.

Slowly, while stifling a loud groan Arida eased herself out of the chair. Her mother had began dozing off, still clasping her father's hands in her own. Arida leaned down and kissed the brow of each of them before walking back through the rooms and into the hallway.

The walk back to her own room was just as quiet as the walk to the kings and queens. It surprised Arida when she looked out the windows they passed to see the sun had already set. Had it been that long? It hadn't felt like the whole day had passed in that bed chamber, but then again, her mother had insisted on leaving the curtains drawn.

A healer had come in at some point and had let them know that in two of the dishes from the fateful breakfast, the mint jelly and the porridge had been laced with high dosages of Strychnine, a poison found in a plant grown commonly in the southern part of Aiden. The healers couldn't answer if her father would make a full recovery or not due to them not knowing how much he ingested before the effects took hold. Whoever had spiked the food was definitely trying to get either one or both of her parents. Arida couldn't shake the feeling of relief of her mother not being there this morning, and guilt over that relief she felt. Her father hadn't gotten any worse throughout the day but he hadn't gotten any better either.

Arida's feet dragged through the door way as she entered her bed chamber. She didn't even look to see if Faelyn followed her or had stayed in his normal position outside the door as she unbuttoned the front of her gown and stumbled towards the bed. The soft thud of the door closing behind her echoed off the stone walls as she shed the light weight garment and left it in a pile on the floor and tipped onto bed to sleep on top of the covers.

Faelyn followed the princess back to her room and was able to grab the door to her chamber and snip it shut before he caught sight of anything as she began disrobing. He had already seen more of the princess than he ever planned on when he had rushed into the bathing room that morning. The number and frequency of the attacks was throwing him and the other members of the royal guard. Though only he knew of the latest one on Arida. Even before he was a part of the princess's private guard, he knew there had been a few attempts on the lives of the royal family over the years of their rule. But none had ever gotten this close, and even fewer attempted again and again so soon. Faelyn ground his teeth together at the memory of the meeting he and Arida had overheard last night. He had yet to tell any of his superiors about the conversation and he was loathe to, for fear of the one he tells being a part of the plot. But he had kicked himself last night and all day today while he stood in that somber room for not stepping out from behind the tapestry in the hallway and getting a look at or confronting the men. Perhaps if he had, his king wouldn't be dying down the hall.

His enhanced hearing picked up the sound of Arida flopping onto the bed through the stone wall. It had been a long, draining day, he too looked forward to his reliever coming in a few hours so he could grab some food and crawl into the small bed in his equally small chamber and get a few hours of sleep. It wasn't long before he picked up the sound of her soft snores, the sound made him smile and chuckle softly.

Faelyn spent the next few hours pacing back and forth in the stone hallway racking his brain trying to figure out who could be behind these attacks and how to keep the queen and princess safe. Obviously, the person behind this had the ability to manipulate not only thugs and assassins but established maids and servants who had loyally served the kingdom for years. They would have to be powerful and influential to be able to do that. Maybe one of the courts lords who was seeking power? Or an established lady, slighted by the royal family? Faelyn hadn't heard rumor of the king being unfaithful to his queen, but he wouldn't be the first monarch to take a lover on the side. But would a jilted lover go this far to take it out on Arida?

Faelyn was deep in his musings when echoing metallic footsteps slowly came towards him. Lifting his head two guards in full armor came up, his relief for the night. Faelyn recognized their faces but didn't know their names. He offered a brief nod which they returned before taking up positions on either side of the door.

He slowly made his way across the hall and down the series of tower stairs to the small chamber room for the princess's private guards on the floor below. Tucked away so as not to be seen, but close enough to respond quickly should the warning bells be signaled.

His room was small but it was all his own. That was one of the privileges of being promoted from a member of the royal guard to one of the family's private security.

Along with the small pay raise and more freedoms in his private time Faelyn reveled in the solitary room. If nothing else than to be away from the constant whispers and stares. Even if he kept his long hair down it was hard to hide his elvish features. The fact he had been able to train and join the guard to begin with showed how far the kingdom had come. After magic failed and seemingly disappeared forever, elves were looked at as no better than creatures after the large host of them had helped Koening during his tirade. Because of the treatment they received, most of the elf population took refuge in their sacred forest, casting off the humans as they themselves were cast off. That forest was where Faelyn had been born, had been raised. And had like very few before him, had left.

He had to believe that things were getting better, that the elves could rejoin the rest of Aiden. That hiding away in their forest was hurting and not helping his people. He had known that the moment he decided to leave he would be shunned by his people, and would be looked at with nothing but hate and suspicion by the humans.

He had trained hard though and eventually found his way working in the castle, starting in the stable cleaning up after the horses and eventually made his way up to soldier. From the day he started in the stables though he was ridiculed, tormented and abused by other members of the court. After he had been promoted to a foot soldier and the man who had ruthlessly tormented him for months finally pushed Faelyn too far in the mess hall one evening a brawl ensued. He had won the fight of course. But there was a punishment for him instigating the fight, as was reported by the senior officers present. He had been shipped off to a city patrol, and it had been months before he had been able to earn his way back to the castle. There were still whispers and snide comments uttered under breaths so low the commanders never heard. Even as he moved his way up the ranks. But all of that ended the day Faelyn was promoted over those same men to serve on Arida's private guard. That was the day he had proven once and for all that even though he was an elf he was a loyal member of the guard and trusted by the queen herself to protect the crown.

Quickly Faelyn removed his gear, placing it on the rack next to his small wardrobe, though his sword stayed next to his bed within arm's reach. His room was an internal one, so there was no windows and no hearth. The surrounding rooms helped warm the stone slightly but Faelyn still wasted no time undressing and quickly crawling into the bed and pulling the covers up to his neck. The winter wool blanket he had layed on top his regular sheets was thick yet scratchy against his bare skin. After the events of the last few days and being with Arida through it all Faelyn hoped he would find sleep quickly. Elves needed less sleep than humans. But after nearly a day and a half without a break Faelyn could feel his body needed rest. But even so he knew he could sleep, eat and be back on guard before Arida woke. Surely the two guards who replaced him could keep her safe until then.

The chill began to fade from the blankets, Faelyn's body heat warming them. His brain still worked at the puzzle of the attacks as he slowly drifted off to sleep.

Chapter Eight

It was late in the morning when Arida rose from bed. She didn't call for a maid as she normally would. The betrayal of the last one setting her up for the attack still to fresh in her mind to ignore. So, she dressed alone. Her long red gown fit oddly without the corset, her long dark hair staying straight and down. Her shoulder ached as she twisted to tie the gowns ribbons on her back. Her headache was better, the swelling of the bump on her head had also gone down. As Arida slipped on her matching red velvet slippers her thoughts strayed to her father. No one had awoken her in the night with news of his passing so Arida was sure he was, at least for the time being, still breathing. She grabbed the large handle on the bedroom door and pulled. Two unfamiliar guards stood at attention in the hall. After a brief pause at the shock of Faelyn not standing there Arida started her way down the hall to the small parlor she used to break her fast every morning.

Some mornings her mother would join her, but today Arida knew she would dine alone. As she made her way down the short hall to the dining room. The steady clanking of the guard's armor moving behind her echoed off the stone. It stuck her as odd that she never noticed that noise when Faelyn walked behind her, now that she thought of it, she never saw him in armor. Just the tunic with the royal seal over top a shirt and leather pants she saw the guards train in. The only thing similar to the guards today was the sword they all carried that hung at their waists. They were standard issue to all the members of the royal guard, but that didn't mean they weren't exquisitely made. Hand forged in the palace's own armory the bright steel always shone as a token of pride to those who wore it, much like the armor the rest of the guard wore. Arida made a mental note to ask the elf why he didn't wear it the next time she saw him.

Though the morning hour was late the small dining table in Arida's private room was still set up with a variety of fruit and pastries. She took a seat at the small ornate table and filled her plate. The guards remained in the hall allowing her privacy to eat unwatched. Without her mother there to keep her company Arida stared out the small window to the front lawn of the palace. The cold grey light pooled into the room, paling the light blue papered walls and reflecting on the various paintings hung up around her. The dining rooms and parlors were the only rooms in the castle that had decorated paper covering the stone walls. When Arida had asked why, her mother's response was that one of her great grandmothers thought the rooms that were used for entertaining and to receive guests should be "dressed" for the part. A small white painted hearth with a fire blazing in it was built on the wall opposite the window and kept the room from growing cold as she sat and leisurely ate a pastry topped in sugar and autumn berries. Though one of her favorites, she hardly tasted it, nor did she really see the scenery out the window which she stared. Her mind wandered towards her father, her mother, and what she was to do. The amulet around her neck had been back to its normal lifeless self. No strange warmth seeped from it even now as she sat by the fire.

Once the food on her plate was gone Arida reached for the small porcelain tea pot seated next to her on the table and made herself a cup of tea. Her eyes watched the clear water slowly turn darker as her tea steeped. Steam wafted up from the cup onto her face. Arida stared blankly down into the cup. Even when the water became so dark it was obvious that it would be too strong and bitter for her liking, she continued just to watch it. Even when steam no longer curled off the top and it had grown cold, she watched it as her brain rolled and turned through all the thoughts and feelings she'd had these last several days. That is until a small voice called her name from the doorway.

Slowly Arida looked up and saw one of the young pages standing in the doorway.

"Go ahead." Arida told him pulling herself up to her full height in her chair and plastering her normal cool look on her face.

"Your highness, her majesty the queen has requested that you handle the daily court appointments today as she doesn't wish to leave the kings side until he awakens." The boy left off the end what Arida knew he was thinking, *or dies*.

"Very well. Thank you." Arida dismissed him, though he didn't bow and take his leave. "Is there anything else?"

"Yes, your highness. I also received a message from your uncle on the way here. He wishes to meet with you in the throne room at your earliest convenience." At that the page did a quick bow and scurried out of the room.

Arida stood from her chair and made it to the door before she paused in front of the guards.

"Where is Sir Faelyn this morning?" She asked to neither one in particular. It struck her as odd he had not joined her yet.

"He was called away to a matter near the gate this morning your highness. We were instructed to be on your guard service until he came to relieve us." The one on Arida's left replied.

"What matter at the gate?" She asked, for no one had told her of any problems. When neither of them replied Arida said more sternly, the coolness of her tone matching the look she still had on her face "What matter at the gate?"

The guard on the right answered this time "Someone was caught attempting to breach the gate this morning my lady. He was shot on site per orders from your uncle after the attempts on your life and the attack on your father the king. As the head of your private guard, Faelyn was sent to resecure the gates and assure no one else will get through."

Arida felt true coldness run through her at the end of the guards telling. *When will this end?* She asked herself before walking past the two men and making her way to the throne room. One of her guards sped up as they neared the door and opened it for her. She nodded her head in thanks as she entered the large room.

Arida paused as she stepped from the hall into the grand room. Normally so full of people, now empty save for her uncle standing up on the dais next to the also empty thrones. Her footsteps clicked against the white marble tile, and echoed off the domed ceiling. Few times in Arida's life had she been in this room and seen the two large thrones front and center empty. Even as a child this room held no appeal to her with no one else in it. Without the people this room seemed too big, too open. The wall of windows allowed the grey light from inside to reflect off all the white stone, giving Arida almost an exposed, out in the open feeling. The pillars stationed around the room partnered with the quiet made Arida feels like she was in some ancient temple, and not in her own home.

Gallis moved down a step from the top of the dais as he saw her enter.

"Good morning, your highness." He said with a slight bow of the head. His grey hair shifting across his usual black cloak.

"Good morning uncle. I came as soon as I got your request to meet. Have you heard anything about father today?" Arida asked moving closer into the room. Only finding it slightly odd that her uncle was so near the thrones without anyone in the room, and why he had requested to meet her in here and not any one of the other rooms or studies.

"All I have heard is that he still lives. He has yet to awaken, and my dear sister has stayed by his side all night. I checked on her late last night before withdrawing to my private chambers. The healers are stumped as to how to cure his, ailment." He moved a two more steps down towards her, though he did not step off the throne's platform completely.

"Hopefully they hear good news and he will be healed quickly." Arida glanced away from her uncle and looked down at her skirts. As a girl her uncle Gallis had hardly paid her any attention. He always floated around the edge of her parents' ears. But whenever she would show up he would lower his gaze to her as if she were no more than an errant fly. It wasn't until the last few years when she began attending royal meetings and received her own throne beside her parents had he began interacting with her. Still not the same as he did with the king and queen but a small comment here, a question there.

"In the meantime," Her uncle continued, "as you are to continue in your parent's stead with court appointments, I thought you may require some help as you have never done so on your own before."

"Thank you, uncle. That is very kind, but unnecessary. I have attended these meetings and held court at my family's side for many years now. I would hate to pull you from your important work." Arida glanced up again. The look on Gallis's face confused her, it was a mix of amusement and frustration. As soon as her gaze locked on his, a small flicker of heat was felt against her chest.

"Believe me dear niece it would be my pleasure to assist you. I have cleared my schedule for the next many weeks in preparation to do so."

"Weeks? My you must not think the healers will not find anything of use then?" The heat began gathering around the amulet, hidden even from her uncle under her gown. Her lack of corset had actually made it easier to hide the bulk of the piece. It also kept it from pressing tightly against her skin. Which meant the heat she was feeling now surely would have been burning her if she had been able to tie a corset strings herself.

"Not at all, it's only when they do find a cure it may take a short time for him to gather his strength and be able to hold court again. And your mother will have her hands full seeing to it that he gets his full strength back. And with you being so young it may be wise to have someone of my years sitting beside you. To guide you through any, rough problems." The smile on his face as he spoke made Arida cringe slightly. His face closely resembled the toads she used to hunt for as a child by the pond when he smiled like that.

Though the smile was disarming she did not miss how he mentioned sitting next to her, not standing by her side as he had done all these years with the king and queen.

"But what of the breach in the gate this morning. I am sure you have much to do getting your men in order to find who is at the root cause of all these attempted attacks." Arida watched as Gallis bristled further. Clearly, he had been informed of the breach, but was unaware that she also knew of it.

"I assure you; I have my best men out there doing just that. I fully trust them to do the work while I assist you with your royal duties." Gallis had slowly stepped back up to the main level on the dais and was now standing in front of King Harland's throne. Positioned just so that one small movement and Arida could almost swear he would take a seat.

Heat flashed again, Arida took a quick glance around the room, looking for any sign of physical attack that the beacon around her neck seemed to be warning against. But there was nothing. It was still only Gallis and herself in the throne room. She returned her gaze to her uncle and studied him closely, noting again how he hovered almost possessively close to the large thrones.

Stealing her spine and trying hard to ignore the warmth building against her skin Arida did her best to emulate her mother when she spoke to her uncle again.

"Truly I do thank you for your offer of assistance uncle. But at this time, I do believe your skills are of better use sniffing out the man behind all the attacks and using your spies to infiltrate any followers he may have grown. So, I must insist upon you not being by my side in my day-to-day proceedings, but I will set up a standing appointment for any findings and updates you may have." At that Arida moved to leave the throne room and proceed to her mother's office where letters and correspondences were waiting for her to read and respond to on the queen's behalf.

"You, *insist*." Gallis hissed out. "How queenly of you, Arida. Your mother would be so proud of the little ruler you are turning into. Her hours of hard work with you and her locked away in her office finally coming in handy."

Arida turned to look at her uncle. Surprised by the anger in his voice. The tone striking a chord in her memory. The memory of a dark hiding spot behind a tapestry, and an irritated voice.

"You know," Gallis continued "I always wondered what you two were doing in there. Your mother always keeping you close, having secret lessons in her office. It always did remind me of how my mother treated Varidia. Secret meetings, whispers and one day that gold chain moving from my mother's neck to Varidia's, just how a few years ago it transitioned from her neck to yours." He paused, eyes tracing the length of chain from where it circled her neck and then plunged below her dress. "That is what peaked my intrigue even more than the meetings I was never allowed to be a part of, even though I was the eldest. No matter how many times I asked, my dear sister would never tell me about that necklace she kept hidden. I thought for sure when it appeared on your neck I would finally find out, but still nothing. Even my best spies couldn't find a hint as to what it could be."

As Gallis took another step down the dais Arida backed up, placing a hand against the bodice of her dress, pressing the pendant against her, the heat scorching even through the fabric.

"It is nothing of importance, I assure you uncle." The queenly tone slipping slightly from Arida's voice. She turned quickly and strode for the large wooden door she had entered in, half tempted to call for her guards.

A dark wind erupted through the room, blowing between Arida and the exit she was headed for. Arida stumbled backwards, shocked by the sudden wind in a room whose windows do not open. Whirling around she stared at Gallis who had one hand lifted, fingers twirling in the same movement as the wind. The amulet flared and burned hot against Arida's skin. She wanted so badly to rip it off and throw it, but she didn't dare. She couldn't risk her uncle seeing it.

"Gallis, what are you doing?!" Arida gasped at the wind whipping across her face, pulling her unbound hair this way and that.

"I am doing what I have too Arida. Your parents have been sloppy with the running of our kingdom. They sit on these thrones and listen to the whining and crying of every villager who sullied the rugs they stood on. Ignoring the call of power that's been building in these lands for centuries. All while I stand in the shadows listening, waiting, faithfully serving. But now I will not sit back and watch the crown pass into the hands of nothing more than a girl who has spent her whole life as her mother's little doll."

There it was, that memory again. Triggered by the only word spoken by both of the mystery men in the hallway that night.

"It was you," Arida said softly. Hardly believing it. "You are the one behind the attacks."

Chapter Nine

"Not as dim witted as you appear, are you?" Gallis laughed. "Yes, it was me. Though I never planned on killing you. My plan was to scare your parents into listening to me about my ideas with integrating magic back into our kingdom. If we are able to harness magic again that would give us an advantage when it comes to disagreements with other kingdoms, a better bargaining chip when the prince's start crawling into the kingdom looking for your hand." Gallis sneered at his last point, Arida shivered at the thought of him having any say in who she married.

"I had hoped that even when it was just the king that fell ill, your mother would be so afraid for your safety and from the attempts made on your life she would insist that I take over the responsibilities of running the kingdom. I thought she would sequester you into her private chambers, as she does every other time. But it appears she has a strange unfaltering faith in your abilities that I just can't seem to see or sway her from."

Gallis took another step towards Arida, the wind he was manipulating growing stronger with the smaller space.

"So now it seems I have to yet again take things into my own hands. At this moment my guards are taking over outside the king and queens bedchamber. Even if the king makes it, they are now my prisoners. And as far as their subjects will be concerned, they both fell ill and are no longer able to do their royal duties. As for you, you will also be kept in your chambers until I find a use for you."

Arida felt a lump of dread twist in her gut. The burning against her skin was so strong tears pricked in her eyes.

"Gallis, I demand you stop this nonsense at once! What you are doing with magic is grounds for execution. I don't even know how you are able to access it in the first place. Let's just forget about this whole incident, it will stay between us. I won't breathe a word about the magic to anyone."

"Magic?" Gallis said looking at Arida with a face splitting smile that reminded her of a spider watching a fly. "How do you know this is magic? Did you not notice the broken window?" Arida followed his gaze to a window in the far corner of the room, mostly hidden from view by one of the many stone pillars, a single pane had been smashed. Arida could see the fluttering of one of the drapes that her mother would have had drawn closed whenever the summer sun would get too strong. He had clearly planned for this. The movement of his fingers meant nothing, something he could have written off easily to anyone if she tried to explain his magic use.

"I, ah ..." Arida was at a loss for words. The amulet burning the hottest it had ever been. Signaling to her the presence of magic and of a spellborn. Her only real tell that it was in fact magic being used, and not his sorry excuse of a broken window. But she couldn't argue and reveal her secret.

"Like I said, sloppy." Gallis was just a few steps from his niece when a commotion could be heard outside the large carved door Arida had used to come in. She turned her head slightly towards the sound.

Gallis used her momentary distraction and lunged for Arida. Grabbing her by the upper arms he began hauling her back towards a small door hidden behind the throne dais. It was the door he always used to slink in and out of without people noticing its location partially covered by another set of long drapes for the neighboring windows. Arida had never been through that door and had no idea where it truly led to.

With as much force as she could muster, Arida began struggling against her uncles hold on her. His grip was surprisingly firm as he continued to pull her, his fingers curling tightly into her skin. The muscles in Arida's arms ached in protest, still sore from her fall. A loud noise echoed again from outside the door, the door that Arida was getting pulled farther and farther away from. But still she struggled against the man who held her.

She dug her heels in but her silk slippers offered no grip against the smooth polished stone.

Just as they were within a few feet of Gallis's secret door the large ones across the room burst open and a swirl of red hair and swords came flying in. Faelyn was fighting toe to toe with one of the members of Gallis's personal guard. Their swords locked with a metallic screech that Arida could feel in her teeth. Shifting to hold the sword in place with one hand the elf punched his now free one into the gut of his assailant earning him a second between attacks to sweep his gaze across the throne room. He paused when he saw Arida, struggling in the grasp of her uncle.

Arida barely had time to get a, "Look out!" yelled across the space before the guard Faelyn had punched stood back up straight, his sword arching up with him as he moved. The elf moved in time to avoid a lethal injury, but still received a gash across his right bicep. Arida let out a gasp at the blood she saw soak through the white shirt he wore under the guard tunic. He gritted his teeth into a snarl, but the injury did not slow him as he struck back.

Arida pulled again at her uncle's grip, hoping the commotion had distracted him, but no luck. The door he was heading for was just a few steps away now. Another one of Gallis's guards came through the door and began grappling with Faelyn. He held his own, two against one for a few swift moments. But Gallis's men were well trained and had been a solid unit for years and each of them had been hand-picked by her uncle for their exemplary skills. It wasn't long until the elf's sword clattered against the stone floor with a noise that echoed through the domed ceiling. As one man grabbed for Faelyn's arms the other reached for the discarded sword and stalked forward. Arida watched helpless as her lone guard struggled against the arm lock hold he was being held in.

Her heart thumped in her chest, the sound echoing in her ears. And suddenly it became all too much, watching the elf struggle just as she did against her own hold. Gallis's second guard stalked towards the men, slowly raising Faelyn's own sword. Preparing to strike what Arida only imagined would be a lethal blow. The fear of what her uncle would do to her once he got her through that door. Plus, the now fiery pain of the amulet searing her skin. The heat so painful she was sure her skin was blistering. It all built and built inside her until it had nowhere else to go. And with a loud battle cry every sense and emotion Arida was feeling came rushing out, in one giant wave of burning power.

Chapter Ten

White light flashed out around her, Arida wasn't sure who all was screaming. If it was just her, the men, or a combination of them all. Energy blasted out with the light, blinding everyone in the room and stopping the assaults. Gallis was blown backwards, his bruising grip releasing Arida in the process. With the sudden release of her arms, blood rushed down into her limbs making them temporarily numb and unable to support her weight as she fell forward. Arida twisted in time, taking the brunt of the fall on her shoulder and hip. Though this time she was able to keep her head from cracking against the floor. As soon as she hit the ground, the white light ceased and the energy died away.

Looking up across the marble floor, Arida could see Faelyn as well as Gallis' guards sprawled across the ground. None of them moving. Small spatters of blood dotted the once pristine floor.

"Faelyn." Arida groaned, trying to prop her arms underneath her. They still felt tingly, as the blood settled back into normal circulation. He shifted on the floor in response to her voice a small groan echoed across the room towards her. Relieved Arida slowly pulled herself back to her feet and moved across the stone floor towards her guard.

His eyes opened when her shadow crossed across his face.

"Are you okay?" Arida whispered, her throat dry and rough from her yell.

"Yeah, I think so." Faelyn replied pulling himself up. He swayed slightly, blood dripping from his arm and tapping on the polished stone. But his movements were still more graceful than Arida's had been.

"What was that?" He murmured, giving Arida a concerned look.

She made to answer but just then, a dark shape began moving in the far corner where Gallis was thrown.

"There's no time, we have to get out of here before they get up." Arida whispered.

Faelyn turned and picked up his sword from where it was dropped, the guard who had previously held it was still not moving. Blood trickled from his nose though making Arida wonder if he ever would. With his sword in one hand Faelyn grabbed Arida's hand with his other and they made their way across the throne room and into the hallway where several more bodies wearing Gallis' colors lay dead.

"You took on all of these men? How did you even know I was in trouble?" Arida exclaimed as Faelyn picked his way across the maze of bodies, leading her around them.

"Like you said, there's no time. We have to get out of here. Come on, this way." Faelyn turned left, moving towards a servant's staircase where they undoubtedly would find an exit from the main palace.

"Wait!" Arida halted, the sudden stop yanking Faelyn back towards her as his grip tightened on her hand to keep from losing it. "My mother, Gallis has them captive. We need to get to their chambers and rescue my mother." Arida felt the deep guilt settle in her at the thought of having to leave her father behind.

Faelyn clenched his jaw, a muscle in his cheek twinged.

"Okay." He said in a resolved tone. "But stay close." He released her hand so he could grip his sword with both of his.

Moving swiftly, they had the good fortune of not running into any other guards until they got to the large wooden door with the eagle in flight, the door to the King and Queens private chambers. Standing outside were a handful of guards also all in the dark black tunics. Faelyn didn't even pause a single step before walking straight toward the party of guards and started swinging his sword in expert strokes and thrusts. Arida stayed hidden around the wall, the sound of steel against steel and the shouting of men echoed towards her. Fear raced through her veins at the amount of sound the fight was making, a calling card for every other guard wearing the wrong color tunic to come this way.

Did any of them still wear red? She thought. But to her relief the rest of the hall stayed empty, not even a maid scurried about.

Arida stayed hidden until the sounds of battle got quieter and quieter. She peaked out and saw her opening. Faelyn already had two guards bleeding out on the floor and was engaging with two more when the last one left guarding the door moved from his post to help the others. As soon as he was far enough away Arida raced for the door. She felt the wet slap of her shoes as she had no choice but to race right through a puddle of blood. But she tried her best to block it out of her head as she creaked the large door open just enough to slip though, not one of Gallis' men noticing her.

She stumbled into the dark entry way of her parents' chambers. The hearth was dark and cold. Clearly no servant had been allowed in to tend to it. She fumbled blindly for something familiar to help lead her way.

"Mother?" Arida whispered.

Her hand finally found a brocade chair that always sat next to the small writing table. Using it as her guide she walked slowly in the direction of a chest of drawers she knew was just past the desk.

"Mother." She whispered again.

"Arida?" Her mother's voice whispered back. A small torch lit up against the darkness of the room and Arida breathed a sigh of relief at the sight of her mother's face.

"Oh mother." Arida rushed forward and landed in her mother's outstretched arm.

"Arida, I am so glad your safe. Gallis was here last night after you left and was saying the most horrible things. I was certain he had you locked away from me somewhere. All of our guards have turned on us, even the ones who have served your father and I for years."

"I know mother, I just escaped Gallis. He used magic and..."

"And?"

"And... I think the amulet did too." Arida saw the color drain from her mother's face.

"I had a feeling Gallis had been hiding something like this for some time now. I just never imagined he would stoop to using magic against his whole family."

"But mother," Arida cried, tears flowed down her cheeks and she grasped at the chain. "I don't know how it did it, one minute the amulet was burning against me skin and I was fighting against Gallis and the next a white light was shining everywhere. It knocked Gallis across the throne room and I was able to get away but I don't know how and..."

"Oh honey," Queen Varidia interrupted, wiping the tears from her daughter's face. "It's okay, this was going to happen eventually."

Arida pulled back, looking at her mother's face "What do you mean it was going to happen eventually?"

Before she could answer the front door burst open and Faelyn barreled in, slamming it shut behind him. Queen Varidia instantly pulled Arida behind her, thrusting the torch grasped in her hands between herself and the elf. Faelyn threw his hands up in an innocent gesture. His sword dangling in his palm.

"Wait mother!" Arida gasped pulling herself forward away from the protective stance "He helped me get away from Gallis, he distracted the guards outside your door so I could sneak through. He's going to help me get you out of here."

Varidia relaxed slightly, looking between her daughter and her guard. She noticed the blood on Faelyn's arm, though the bleeding had slowed it was still pooling into his shirt and tunic.

"Here, come with me and we will get you all fixed up." The queen led them through the chambers and into the small bathing room. Arida glanced towards the bed and felt a mixture of sadness and relief at the still figure laying under the sheets. Still breathing but still unconscious.

The queen grabbed a small rag from a neatly folded pile on a marble table and walked across the room to a small inlet in the wall where water flowed freely through the rock and down into a small basin where it drained back to its natural stream. Arida always loved the little waterfall as a child, it was pretty to watch the candlelight flicker in its stream, and it was large enough to offer a gentle relaxing ambient noise to the stone room. Varidia got the cloth wet and then slowly cleaned the wound on Faelyn's arm. The gash was long but shallow and once she deemed it clean enough, she took another rag from beside her and ripped a strip away from it forming a makeshift bandage to bind the wound tightly. Silently she got up and disappeared back into the bed chamber before returning with a white shirt that looked similar to the one Faelyn had been wearing.

"Here." She said handing it over. "It's one of Harland's' but he wont mind."

Faelyn smiled in thanks and turned to begin taking off the soiled tunic and shirt. The queen left the bathing room again and gestured for Arida to follow. Arida fought the urge to turn around when she heard the soft sound of fabric hitting the stone floor. After all, she mused, he had seen her in far less. But instead she studiously followed her mother back into the bed chamber where the queen stopped at her husband's bedside and took his limp hand in her own.

"Now Arida listen closely." Her mother whispered in a tone she only assumed she was using in hopes the elf in the next room couldn't hear over the running water. "That necklace as you know is passed down to the first daughter of every blood line for protection." Arida nodded. "The piece was created by your ancestor when she was just a princess, not much older than you are now. One thing history lost over time was that she was Spell-born, and a powerful one. That is why Koening kept her close to him during her imprisonment. He leeched off the remnants of her power, using her as his own personal supply whenever he needed it. Collete was able to create the amulet in secret, how we don't know. But she formed it into a talisman, an object imbued with power. And when the time came, she used all of her power, channeled through the magic of the talisman and sealed off access to all magic. Good and bad. It was the only way to stop Koening from using it. The only power left was in the amulet, but only enough to work like a warning bell. To alert Collete's descendants if power began to reawaken. Because on the day Koening was defeated his body had become so accustomed to feeding of the remnants of power of others that when it was cut off completely, he began to fade. He had become a leech without a host. But magic, though blocked to its users wasn't gone from everywhere. And because of that, a small part of him continues to live on in a way.

So, because of that the amulets power useful in keeping the line safe, by alerting us if magic is being used nearby to the wearer. You have felt this when it heats up, and that happens always in the presence of magic. So, with the benefits of its warning also comes the responsibility of locating the Spellborn its warning you of. As you know we were to extinguish them immediately to keep Koening from being able to feed off their power and coming back into his own." The queen stared at her daughter, watching her try to absorb all of the information being thrown at her. This was it, another piece to the puzzle that Arida had been trying to construct.

So, the amulet was capable of more. Could it too be trying to reawaken? Was that what had just happened moments ago in the throne room?

She was trying to figure out how to phrase the part about their final moments in the throne room and to tell her mother about how she got away form Gallis when Varidia spoke again.

"The hardest part of ruling is sacrificing the few for the good of the many." Her mother reached forward and tucked a stray hair behind her ear. Arida was confused as to what she meant and was about to aske when Faelyn reappeared in his new fresh shirt. All hints of blood wiped away from his hands as well.

In an instant Varidia switched from concerned mother, back to the queen of Aiden as she took in the elf.

"We need to get going, we are running out of time before someone notices the bodies piled up outside the door." He adjusted his sword belt in a sign of nervousness.

"Come" The queen ordered standing quickly. "This way." She ushered them out of the bed chamber and into the small private library. Arida paused for a moment before leaving the bedroom to kiss her father's cheek and to give one of his large hands a gentle squeeze. She wished there was some way to protect him too. But with one final squeeze she let go and followed her mother.

Varidia walked past the hearth, the fire long dead in it, past the bookcases and over to the far wall where a large tapestry hung. Like the other night with Faelyn, the queen pushed the tapestry back and uncovered not another hiding spot, but a small door.

"Mother, what is this?" Arida asked, surprise in her voice.

"This is a hidden passage, another one of Collete's ideas after the ordeal of being held hostage by Koening for years, she wanted to make sure that never happened to another one of her descendants ever again. So, she had this hidden passage placed in the royal bed chamber." Quickly the queen twisted the door handle and pushed gently against it. With a quiet creak the door opened to reveal a narrow set of stairs leading down. No torches lit the way, nothing but dust coated the stone stairs.

"There are a few others around the castle, but this one I traveled down once, after my own mother told me of their existence. It leads down and out away from the castle. At the end is a small cave entrance hidden by foliage that opens up just outside the village of Clarea. There you should be able to get horses and supplies to flee." The queen pressed a small coin bag into Arida's hand. "This should be enough to get you far from here, if you are careful with it."

It was at this point her mother's words had sunken in and Arida realized her mother had no plans of going with her.

"Wait, what about you? We came here so you could come with us." Tears were once again building in the edges of Arida's eyes. He mothers face grew sad and she reached a hand up and cupped her daughters face.

"I know my love. But I must stay here. If I leave, there is no one left who will guard your father. He has yet to awaken but I hope soon he will." Tears now slid down both mother and daughter's face. "As soon as he wakes up, you will find us, right? And then we can figure out how to take the kingdom back from Gallis." Arida's voice wavered. She glanced over to where her father laid motionless. The only sign the once larger than life man was even still alive was the silent sound of his breathing that she could still hear from this side of the chamber.

"Exactly, we will find you wherever you go." Queen Varidia leaned forward and pressed a kiss to Arida's forehead. A sad smile was on her face as she Leaned back. She looked towards Faelyn who had been keeping a close but respectful distance from them.

"You keep my daughter safe." It was an order from a queen if there ever was one. Faelyn even bowed in response.

"With my life, your majesty."

The queen handed him the torch and motioned for him to start down the stairs. With both hands free she fully enveloped her daughter in a hug. Squeezing her tightly.

"Trust your instincts, they will always be right." Pulling back, she looked her daughter in the eye and brushed a stray hair from her face. "You are so strong, and I know wherever you go, you'll be okay."

"I love you mother." Arida whispered.

"Oh, I love you too Arida. Be brave my girl." And with that the queen ushered her princess to follow her guard. It wasn't until the last flickers of the torches' reflection faded off the wall did the queen shut the door tightly, let the tapestry fall back into place and retake up her post at her King's side once more.

Chapter Eleven

The tunnel stairs were old, but sturdy. The pair walked down slowly, nothing but the sound of scuffing shoes and the swish of Arida's skirts echoed inside the stairwell. The stairs went on and on, seemingly without end. After close to half an hour of descending the stone steps they eventually leveled out into a packed dirt path, the even stone brick walls began to show irregularities in the construction. As Arida followed Faelyn further down the tunnel, the flames from the torch reflected against the brick as it slowly turned into the solid rock formation of a cave.

After close to another half an hour a muted light glowed from up ahead, an opening to the cave. As they got closer to it, Arida could see the shapes of plants and vines growing across the opening, concealing it from those who may walk by from the other side. Faelyn snuffed the torch out against the dirt floor before moving to shift some of the plant life out of the way.

With minimal breakage he was able to make a small passage between the vines and a large green bush. He held his hand up for Arida to pause as he ducked through and checked around to make sure there were no surprises waiting for them on the other side. After a few silent seconds, Faelyn reappeared and pulled the plants aside again, motioning for Arida to follow.

The skirts of her red gown, though without their usual extra layers underneath still proved difficult to squeeze through the brush. Even with Faelyn's help Arida had to pull and tug herself through. The thick material snagging and catching on every twig. When she was finally free, she looked down and noticed several rips and tears in the fabric.

"We are going to have to find you something more sensible to wear when we reach Clarea. We won't be going anywhere fast if I have to pull you out of every plant in Aiden we come in contact with." Faelyn said looking

Arida up and down. Though he was right, Arida still felt her spine stiffen under his thorough inspection.

"What direction do we go in now?" She asked trying to smooth out her skirts to hide the stray threads poking out.

"The first buildings for town are just over the hill that way." Faelyn pointed straight ahead where the land began to incline, trees blocking Arida's view of the afore mentioned buildings.

"The sun is going to be setting in a few hours." Faelyn looked toward the horizon, shielding his eyes from the bright light. "We need to be quick in town. Get in and get out while the sun is still far enough in the sky we can get some distance. Once Gallis knows your gone this will be the first place he comes." He turned and looked at Arida.

"Besides, you are surely to be recognized here, and we can't risk anyone alerting your uncles guards that you made it out of the castle. We need to gather the supplies we need and leave."

"Where will we go after?" Arida asked, the knowledge of what they had just done, and what they were about to do was starting to make her head spin.

"I'm not sure. We will camp in the woods on the other side of Clarea, get some distance between us and the castle. And then, just figure it out from there I guess."

Faelyn studied Arida's, the mask of the princess had slipped slightly. Her cheeks were still tear stained; her hair slightly tangled. She held his gaze until he turned and started up the slight hill separating them from the town.

Arida stumbled and slipped many times on their trek up the hill. Though not steep, her red velvet slippers had been meant for polished marble and stone floors, not grass and mud. That coupled with her cumbersome skirts slowed their progress greatly.

By the time she made it to the tree Faelyn waited by for her, her brow had a fine sheen of sweat and her breaths were coming out in small gulps.

"You know?" Faelyn said with a wry smile at the princess as she slumped into a sitting position, as best as she could. "The next time you decide to fight off your uncle and then run for it, can I recommend changing first? Or perhaps doing some cardio?"

Arida fumed as she glared up at the elf.

"You know, I am still your princess and you really should speak to me with a little more respect."

Faelyn chuckled "We should really get a move on *your highness*. You know, if you want to make it to the shops *before* they close." At that he turned and started strolling into the trees, leaving Arida still sitting in the grass.

Clumsily she got to her feet and followed him into the trees. The whole time hoping a squirrel would throw a pine cone right on his head. She thought for a split second her wish had been answered when Faelyn stooped down, but then he just grabbed a long blade of grass that was growing around the trunks of the large pine trees they were walking under, and plucked it in-between his teeth.

Brambles and bushes snagged and tugged at her gown as she walked after her guard. The irritations, though small were making her blood boil. She was just about to figure out a way to tie the yards of fabric up, when Faelyn paused. Looking up, Arida could see the outline of a building right in front of them.

"If anyone asks after your appearance, we say you were out on a ride on your horse and the animal was spooked and you fell off. You were trying to walk back to the castle when I was out on patrol and found you. That will cover as to why we are asking for clothes and horses. They will assume I am trying to get you back to the castle quickly."

Arida nodded, though she was irritated about his story, it was a good one. It reasoned why she was looking the way she was and the townspeople would not question helping her return to the castle like they would if they knew she was fleeing.

The elf turned and again gave Arida a once over look.

"I say we secure horses first, then move on to supplies and clothes."

They stared at each other for a moment before approaching on the edge of the forest. Arida made sure her cool, stoic face she wore in court was frozen onto her face as she walked a step behind Faelyn's shoulder. The blade of grass tossed aside into the dirt path behind them.

Chapter Twelve

T he town of Clarea was moderate in size. Small
enough that it shouldn't take long to run all their
errands and get out before anyone could grow suspicious over Arida's timing in town. After all she rarely
was permitted out of the castle. And when she was it
was always with both of her parents and a large en-
tourage of guards. But the town was large enough that
when the first stable they went to asked a ridiculous
amount of money for two subpar brown mares, Faelyn
had several other stables to barter with. When they had
two horses purchased and held to be fully tacked up for
them, they still had plenty of coin left for Faelyn to hand
some over to Arida to find new attire while he went into
the village's food market to gather the remaining supplies for their journey. He seemed confident that Gallis's

men would still be searching the palace for them, unaware of their quick hidden exit. And his plan to divide and conquer would get them out of town faster.

Arida walked down the packed dirt road, peaking through the shop windows she passed. Careful not to look any of the shop keepers in the eye for too long. It had crossed her mind after she nodded at the first one and he had given her an odd look that many of these people could have come to court to request and were denied, making them no fans of hers.

Clarea relied heavily on the palace for everything. Whether it be for assistance with food or their living situations or a dispute between neighbors they turned to their monarchs for help, a perk of being just outside the palace walls. But sometimes they were turned away to deal with smaller problems and squabbles themselves. Some of which found this to be a shirking of the palace's responsibilities and were scorned from it.

When she finally looked into one shop and saw an adequate selection of clothing for travelers just inside the window she ducked in through the wooden door.

The shop keeper was a young woman with a mane of sandy curly hair who smiled warmly at her when she entered. Arida nodded in return before turning toward one of the tables that had a variety of dark leather boots placed neatly in a row. It was at this point that Arida realized she didn't have the faintest idea what shoe size she wore. Her clothes and shoes were always purchased for her by one of her clothiers. Any items that didn't fit perfectly, were tailored too. Arida didn't even know where to begin.

"Is there something I can help you with?" A soft voice asked behind her.

Arida startled and whirled around. The shop keeper, having seen her staring at the boots for longer than normal had moved from behind her counter and come over.

"I uh, yes. I am going to be traveling a little differently than I am used to, so I am going to be needing some clothes more... appropriate for traveling a long distance. But..." Arida paused, suddenly embarrassed that she was even asking for help.

"But... you don't know what to get?" The shop keep finished. Arida just nodded.

"Okay, no problem." The young woman looked Arida up and down. "So, you'll certainly need some nice boots." She turned and grabbed a pair off the table, handing them over to Arida. They were well made out of a firm dark brown leather that would go up just past her ankle. They had thick dark laces that would secure them snuggly in place. The textured grip at the bottom made it clear these were made for traveling and not for fashion.

"Next, here is a leather jerkin, and a tunic to go under it." The woman pulled pieces seemingly at random from stacks around her shop and passed them over her should.

Arida stacked the clothing the girl handed her on top of her boots and followed her to the next area of the shop. She was thankful no one else was in there but her. The keeper rifled through a small stack of what looked to be leather items before unfolding a pair and revealed them to be a leather legging. They reminded Arida of the ones Faelyn always wore and she couldn't put her finger on why, but the sight of them made her oddly happy. When the woman handed those over, she rubbed the material near the waist between her thumb and finger and found that they were indeed a dark brown leather exterior but they had a soft lining to make them warmer and more comfortable. Arida looked up and noticed the shop owner had moved again and was digging through a stack of smaller items on a small circular table. As Arida got closer she noticed that it was a table of under-clothes and a few of the small pieces found themselves stacked on top of her armful.

"Now," The shopkeeper said, leading her to a small area in the back of the store that had a curtain pulled halfway open. "You can go ahead and try these things on in here. I will be at the counter when you are ready." Arida thanked her before closing the curtain and began unbuttoning the front of her gown.

She slowly shimmied out of her gown and chemise, letting them pool on the ground at her feet. Arida paused for a moment and stared at her blood-stained slippers before slowly using the toe of one to slide the other off. She kicked them under the pool of fabric to hide them away. The tunic and Jerkin went on and laced in the front to a perfect fit. The leggings were snug and foreign. Though still covered by material, Arida felt like the bottom half of her body was exposed to everyone. She unrolled a pair of soft thick socks and slipped them over her feet before unlacing the boots and putting them on, another perfect fit. Arida wasn't sure how the shop keeper was able to perfectly fit her; especially in the state her gown had been in. The shirt and the pants she could have chalked up to just having a good eye and being able to do her job very well, but her feet... her feet had been covered by her skirts the whole time she was in the store.

Arida stooped down and picked up her gown off the floor and carefully folded the soiled shoe in the folds of the fabric. She then double checked that the amulet was well hidden before pulling the curtain back. The shop-keeper was exactly where she had promised she would be, behind her counter. Arida looked at her closely, the woman had to be no older than Arida herself. And she didn't seem to hint that her princess was standing in her store.

Arida moved forward to the front counter.

"Everything fit okay?" she asked and smiled warmly.

"Yes, thank you. How much do I owe you for all of this?" Arida reached toward the pocket in her jerkin where she had stuffed the coins Faelyn had given her.

"Three silvers will cover it all. For four silvers I can also add in a riding cloak. It's far too cold to be out traveling without one."

"Oh, yes please." Arida replied, fishing another coin form her pocket. "That's a good idea. Say, would you mind getting rid of this for me?" Arida lifted her gown, the small tears almost more noticeable now at eye level, and placed it on the counter along with the four silver coins.

"Absolutely. This was a beautiful piece milady, it's a shame to see it in the state it's in." Pulling the gown across the counter, she placed a black woolen cloak in its place.

"Yes, I'm afraid the gown was not meant for a hike through the woods." Arida pulled the cloak over her shoulders and clasped it. "It's too bad too, it was one of my favorites."

"Yes, the stitching is beautiful, and the fabric... unique." The shop keeper gave Arida a look.

"Yes, it is." Arida said, suddenly felling like she should be careful with her words.

"You know, my sister made a gown very similar to this one. She had even imported the fabric special. She worked for days to get the details just right. I think I watched her redo the trim around the collar three times so that it laid just so. Because that dress went to the Princess Arida." The woman brushed her hand along the top of the fabric, smoothing the threads that stuck up loosely. "I sometimes assist my sister with her gown shop down the street. And though I've never met her highness I've assisted in creating many of her gowns."

Arida had froze, that explained how she was able to pick out all the correct sizes. The sister she spoke of

Arida knew well. Many of her dresses in fact were made by her, the woman had a gift for dress making.

"Please." She whispered, though there were no other people in the shop.

"Don't worry your highness, I won't tell a soul. When I saw you in the state you were in, I figured if you wanted people to make a fuss about your appearance, you'd have announced it."

Arida couldn't speak for a second. She glanced out the window and noticed Faelyn crossing the road towards her, a large pack looped on one shoulder, and a saddle bag slung across the other.

Turning back to the woman Arida said "I thank you for not telling anyone. You have no idea. And please, if any guards come by asking..."

"I never saw you." She replied with a straight stern face. " And it was my pleasure to help you your highness. I wish you safe travels, wherever they may be."

"Thank you again, you look after yourself." Arida nodded at the shopkeeper before turning and exiting the shop.

Chapter Thirteen

B y the time Arida left the shop, the sun was sinking behind the buildings and trees, casting dark shadows into the street and allies. When she got to where Faelyn was waiting for her, he ran his cursory glance over her. Arida once again got that exposed feeling when his eyes landed on her legs.

"Nice." Was the only comment he deigned to make.

"Thank you." She replied curtly. "Did you get everything you needed?" She then noticed he too now wore a thick cloak that was secured around his neck. And it wasn't just one set of saddle bags slung over his shoulder, but two. One had been stacked on top of the other, packed and balanced perfectly so as not to tip.

"Yes, and we have plenty of gold pieces, and a couple of coppers left. Now we should really get back to the stable and get ready to leave town. I don't want to stay here any longer than we need to. Though without the gown, your far less recognizable. I know if I saw you walking around town I wouldn't think you were the princess."

Arida nodded, unsure how else to respond to that comment and followed Faelyn down the somewhat crowded street towards the public stable. A groom stood outside near two horses that were saddled and waiting. Both were light brown and hardly anything special.

"Better to blend in" Faelyn whispered in response to the obvious disappointment in their mounts that must have been all over Arida's face. She quickly cleared it, making her expression blank and bored.

"As long as they are able to get us where we need to be, I don't care what they look like." Though the memory of her pure white stallion she was gifted for her birthday a few years ago flashed briefly through her mind. He definitely was more than capable of getting her places quickly.

With her new pants Arida found mounting the brown mare she was given far easier than she'd ever experienced. The close hugging fabric allowed for her leg to swing over quickly, unencumbered by the yards and yards of skirts she normally wore. After she was settled in her saddle, Faelyn attached one of the sets of saddle bags he had flung over his shoulder to the back end of her horse. He secured them tightly to the saddle, and tugged at the straps to confirm they weren't going anywhere before moving on to secure the second set of bags to his own horse.

Arida lifted the top flap on one of the bags now draped behind her. There were various items tucked neatly inside. Arida picked up one of the small pouches and discovered it full of something small and shriveled. She carefully plucked one of the brownish orange pieces up and twisted it in her fingers. Arida thought it may at one time had been a nectarine, she quickly dropped it back into the pouch and cinched it up.

"I believe the food you purchased has already turned." She said after discovering another pouch full of another shriveled up item. This one a dark brown color.

Faelyn chuckled. "It's not turned, it's been dried. I know your used to fresh fruit every day up in your shiny palace. But down here where we may go months in between shipments, people learn to dry their fruit so that it lasts longer." He turned having finished tightening the saddle bag straps on his horse. "If we ration it right, we won't have to stop in any town near here. There are also strips of dried pork and a few portions of nuts. The only thing we will have to keep an eye out for is water. We have a couple flasks, but if we try to carry to much it'll just weigh down the horses and we won't move as quickly."

Arida gazed down into the saddle bag she still had propped open and did in fact see a small sleeve with long dark strips of meat that were equally as shriveled as the strange nectarine. And a lumpy bag that she assumed contained the nuts. She resecured the small latch on the bag before grabbing a hold of her reins.

Faelyn swung himself into his saddle with a grace that only elves seemed capable of mastering. After he was seated, he also did a cursory look around his horse before grabbing the reins and motioning his head in the direction he slowly moved his horse into. Arida tapped her heels against the mare's side and followed suit.

Chapter Fourteen

If Arida thought it had been cold in town, it was nothing compared to when their horses stepped on to the road covered in a canopy of tree branches. Without the small warmth the sun provided, Arida quickly felt her fingers chill around the reins she clasped now wishing she had grabbed some gloves as well. Though she had never been this far into the forests, primarily staying in the small well-kept groves directly around the palace, she was still familiar with the hushed tones you only could get while under tree cover. Everything seemed to calm once you entered the forest. The birds chirped more peaceful melodies, the wind whispered through the branches, slowly dying out in strength before reaching them and only dancing lightly through their hair. Even the horses hoofbeats didn't seem to cause as loud of a thud, even though they were still on the hard packed road that they left Clarea on.

Arida pulled her cloak a little tighter around her, hoping to keep more of her body heat close. Hopefully, she thought, she would grow accustomed to the bite of the cold and it wouldn't sting as much.

Faelyn had the horses trotting along at a speed that was slow enough not to attract attention, but quick enough that soon they passed the last small house on the outskirts of the village. Now the only people they would pass on the road were either fellow travelers, or Gallis's guards.

At the thought of her uncle Arida shivered again.

They rode in silence, with Faelyn in the lead for about a mile until he slowed his horse to a stop and waited for her to join him.

"We'll go off the trail here. Hopefully anyone following will lose our tracks and turn around before we re-enter the road further down."

Arida turned and looked into the woods in front of them. The trees were closer together, with thick foliage growing in between the large trunks. Everything was still so green despite the cold, it gave the forest a permanent damp look. It definitely would be hard to follow their tracks through all of that, but that also meant riding for however long Faelyn thought was acceptable would most surely not be easy either.

But Arida had been taught to be strong by the very woman she had left behind in that castle. So, she sat up straight and readjusted her frozen fingers onto the reins of her horse.

"After you." Was her only response.

Faelyn studied her for half a second, but he read nothing but cool indifference on his princess's face. He turned and guided his horse into the forest, not looking back to see the first of many tree limbs brushing against Arida's face. The trees didn't just look like they were wet, they were wet. The autumn sun being unable to penetrate through the thick canopy throughout the day, never burning off the accumulation of morning dew and evening rain. The water droplets sprinkled from the needles and leaves causing a whole new level of discomfort Arida had never experienced. The whisps of hair around her face clung to her chilled skin, her cloak was slowly getting a glistening sheen to it as well. Though no moisture had seeped through it. She'd have to compliment the shopkeeper on her choice... if she ever went back. Though her body was relatively dry the constant feeling of wet on her exposed skin was becoming increasingly irritating to deal with. But like when she was first learning how to live with the weight of the amulet constantly around her neck and tucked into every corset, she gritted her teeth and silently bore it.

Following the elf deeper and deeper into the forest, she wasn't sure if her eyes would ever adjust to the constant dusk lighting. The only thing that stood out against the green was Faelyn's bright red hair. If it wasn't for that she wasn't sure if she would have been able to spot him at certain times when his mare got too far ahead of her own. Their all brown color appearing to be a wise choice after all, the perfect camouflage in the forest. Her stallion would have been far more noticeable than the soft brown bodies that carried them.

Their horses weaved in and out of the trees with ease. Faelyn guided them through as if there was a path that only he could see. Many times, Arida wanted to ask how on earth he knew where they were going. But her imagined responses from him were enough to irritate her into biting her tongue. After all Faelyn in real life was far more irritating than Faelyn in her head.

Slowly, the hours passed. Arida was aware of the forest growing darker around them. Trees she was once able to see farther than twenty yards were now becoming undefined dark shadows. The birds she had heard and sometimes seen flitting around the tree canopies had begun to hush. It had grown eerily quiet in the moments before true nightfall. Arida made sure her horse stayed as close to her guards as she could get it. She had also noticed Faelyn's head moving back and forth as if he was searching for something. It eventually dawned on her that elf eyesight was far superior to her own human eyes, and therefor he probably could still see around them as clearly as if dusk were still hours away.

Suddenly he veered his horse off to the right, cutting it though a patch of tall grass and shrubbery. Arida made to pull her own reins and follow but her horse was already turning, clearly knowing it was to follow her companion. After the horses cleared the brush, they curved around a grove of shorter, more bush like trees and walked out into a small clearing. Perfectly tucked away where anyone with normal human vision wouldn't see if they had been following the small trails their horses had left.

As soon as Faelyn dismounted his horse Arida quickly followed. Relieved to finally be out of the saddle. Her legs were sore from riding for so long, especially since because she was wearing pants now. She hadn't ridden in her traditional side saddle way and the new position had strained her muscles in ways she was not used to. Her knees buckled slightly from the impact when she hit the ground, her teeth clenched tight in an effort to stifle the groan trying to escape.

Faelyn, unfazed from the hours on horseback went to work, silently pulling items out of his saddle bags. After he had a small pile of gear at his feet did, he glance at Arida.

"Why don't you start trying to find some dry fire wood while I set up camp." He stated before turning to the horses and tugging at the straps to their bags. Arida's cheeks burned at the feeling of being chastised as she stiffly turned and wandered back into the tree line to try and find wood for their fire. Thudding sounds of packs hitting the ground followed her.

Arida flexed her stiff fingers as she reached for several branches. Now away from the elf and any other prying eyes she let the silent tears she had been holding in since saying good bye to her parents roll down her cheeks as she worked at her small task. Though she would make sure to have them dry and undetectable before she returned. But for now, she let them go.

Chapter Fifteen

When his niece had shown up in the throne room that morning Gallis had no idea that the events of the day would unfold as they did. How on earth had she learned to wield magic? And how had he known nothing about it? After he had pulled himself off the throne room floor and found two of his guard's unconscious and the rest of them dead, he quickly shut down every part of the castle he could. After getting reports of Arida's chamber empty, and no sign of her or that elf guard showing up at any exits he had quickly gone to his sisters' chambers. Upon finding even more dead guards he had pulled a shield of magic around himself before entering the dim chambers of the king and queen. He had no idea Arida could use magic, so it would then lead him to believe his sister could as well.

Upon finding the queen still dutifully at her king's side Gallis questioned her about the princess's whereabouts. Though Varidia was adamant to know what he had done with her daughter and said she hadn't seen her since her daughters visit the night before Gallis had a feeling his sister was lying to protect her. He had attempted to scare her into telling him where Arida was by threatening to lock her away from seeing her dying husband, but she would not budge.

Gallis knew of a few secret tunnels here and there around the castle. He had discovered them as a child, a small benefit of growing up alone and excluded from the private lessons his sister attended with their mother. They now were used to get his spies around unseen. But whether or not his niece or her irritating guard knew of their existence he had no clue. So, he stationed his men at every exit both know to the rest of the palace and unknown. He knew eventually the princess or her guard would show up.

But as the morning turned into afternoon and there were no signs of them. Even after having the whole castle searched numerous times. He knew then they must have gotten by him and his men somehow. He had half a mind to drag Varidia out of her chamber and lock her in a dungeon until she told him where the girl had gone. But she was so stubborn he knew before he even wasted his time that she would never break. And the last thing he wanted was for servants to see him dragging their queen through the palace. All of the events so far would prove hard enough to explain away. Arida must have escaped through a passage he had yet to discover.

The next closest place they could have gone was Clarea, the small peasant town just outside the palace. Gallis decided to take several of his guards on a short horseback ride beyond the castle walls. He kept his gaze alert the whole way, looking for signs of the pair. But his bird like eyes picked up no sign of anyone traveling by foot or horse recently.

The town square was small and dusty. Centered around a half-filled water feature fed by the run off of the natural spring the palace had been built on top of. The town took advantage of the freshwater to sustain them. And the support of the surrounding farms the palace paid to maintain kept them fed. But it didn't stop the villagers from lining up every week to express their complaints and woes.

Gallis stood by the small fountain letting his horse drink straight from the water well, surrounding the springs stream as his men searched the shops and homes. They questioned the villagers one by one to see if any of them had seen the princess. It was on Gallis's orders that they shared that the princess and her rogue elven guard were wanted for the attempted murder of King Harland. And anyone who had been found to help them without stepping forward now would be punished for treason. It was how Gallis had been able to explain away all the blood and bodies of his guards that the elven filth had left behind from his escape with Arida.

He watched as his men moved from shop to shop. It was when one started forward towards him with a man from the stables on his tail that Gallis felt a small rush of victory.

"Sir, this man says he supplied horses to an elf and a woman who matched the Princess Arida's description." The guard stepped to the side so Gallis could see the stable man. He was short and slight, dressed in clothes a step above rags. His smell alone told Gallis he worked with horses.

"Honest, sir." The man stammered "I didn't know it was the princess. I... I... mean she didn't look like a princess. The elf just asked if he could buy two fresh horses and have them saddled while they picked up supplies." The man was wringing his hands in worry.

"Did he say where they were headed next?" Gallis asked, his voice hissing out like a frustrated snake whose mouse just got away. Arida was a decent rider, with fresh horses they could easily be halfway to the next town by now if they stuck close to the roads.

"No... No... sir. Honest, they didn't mention it." The man was trembling so hard now the small pieces of hay that poked off his clothes even shook.

Gallis waved the man off and watched as he scurried back to his stable. He turned then to his guard. "If they were buying supplies that means others here were helping them. I want you to gather the shop keepers and bring them to me now." He glowered at some of the towns people that scurried away from him. Going back to their closed shuttered homes in hopes of hiding from his obvious irritation.

His guard bowed once and then walked quickly to where his comrades were still patrolling around the small buildings on the main road. At a bark of commands, they all split and walked into the shops.

One by one they all reappeared, dragging a shopkeeper toward the town square. There was one in particular that got Gallis's attention. She had come out of the clothing shop and wasn't quivering in fear the way the other store owners were. She walked sternly, and when they came to a stop in line with the others she jerked, pulling her arm from the guard's grip.

Gallis looked her up and down. The woman was dressed well even for a shop keeper. As he raked his eyes over her once more, she crossed her arms and gave him a withering look. Unbeknownst to her, the hostility that was radiating off of her was exactly the tell he was looking for. The other shop owners cowered beside her making her despisal that much more apparent.

"Tell me miss, did you happen to see her royal highness today?" Gallis said, his voice slithering out like a shadow on his tongue as he stepped closer to the woman.

"I'm quite sure *sir*, I have never seen the princess so I therefor would never know if I ever did meet her."

Her answer rang with enough vague truth Gallis couldn't help but appreciate it. She would have done well in court should she have been born a class or two higher.

And though he appreciated her wording finesse Gallis's mood was quickly turning from amused to not at the shopkeepers' unhelpful attitude, reminding him a lot of his niece. But before he could open his mouth again Gallis was interrupted by one of his men.

"Sir!" The guard called out as he made his was from an alley that wrapped its way behind the line of shops and opened up just in front of the small group of shopkeepers. He had a large piece of some kind of dark red fabric in his hands. Fabric that looked vaguely familiar. "I found this stashed away in a bin behind a clothing shop."

As the guard came closer Gallis was able to tell the material wasn't as shapeless as it originally appeared. And it was in fact a gown... a gown that Arida had been wearing earlier that day.

"Now, what is that doing back there." He rubbed his hand down the fabric, it was cool and damp like it had been in that alley for several hours. It's once smooth embroidered design now rough with loose threads and dirt. "How could a young lady show up in a gown of this make, in a hovel of a town like this..." Gallis lifted his eyes to the lineup of people shivering in front of him. "And go completely unnoticed? Surely someone recognized their princess. And perhaps one thought to render aid?" He tried softening his voice at the end, hoping a merciful tone would loosen some lips.

Under the gaze of the kingdom's head of security the shoe cobbler lost bladder control, earning a look of disgusted happiness from the man forcing them all there.

"Perhaps she changed before coming into the *hovel* and stashed the gown there before anyone could notice." The woman in front of Gallis spoke up. Still leering at him, but now with a slight edge.

"Perhaps indeed." He stepped away and slowly circled her. "Or perhaps someone thought if they hid the evidence long enough to burn it in their evening fire, no one would ever know that they helped the princess escape after she attempted to murder her father the king."

The shop keeper lifted her chin a little higher but said nothing in return. A small crowd of villagers had started congregating nearby. Most wore curious yet weary looks on their faces. But there was one woman mingling in the crowd who caught Gallis's attention for two reasons. The first was the look of complete devastation she wore as she stared down the defiant shop keeper in front of him. And the second was, he recognized her.

Sometimes people from the village frequented the halls of the castle, those with certain skills the royals found useful. Smiths, exceptional bakers, and one that was most popular with the queen and princes... a dressmaker. And that very dressmaker who Gallis had witnessed coming and going from his sister and niece's chambers dozens of times was the very woman standing just off to the side of the rest of the crowd ringing her hands in a worried motion and staring down the woman keeper who bore a striking resemblance to her.

Sweeping his gaze over the others gathered before him he also noticed there was a small man in an apron near the end who was also nervously looking at the woman shopkeeper. His gaze would dart from her to the ground in front of him, the whole while his knees were practically knocking together. Clearly a man who knew something, Gallis used this as his moment.

"I am offering a one-time immunity to the first person who can tell me where the princess and her guard headed." Gallis paused in front of the apron clad man and pulled a coin from his pocket. Holding it between his finger and thumb just at the man's eye level. "I will also add a gold piece onto that if the person also knows who aided in her escape." His eyes slid back to the nervous man who looked one more time at the woman before peering up and meeting Gallis's gaze.

"She took off into the woods near the end of town." The man stammered, knees knocking harder than ever. How they stayed supporting him Gallis would never know. "They took off a few hours ago on horseback."

Gallis nodded as he strolled closer to the man. He flicked the coin casually in the air and caught it, holding it out again with an enticing open palm.

"You wouldn't happen to also know who stashed that dress in the alley would you?" Gallis said slowly and calmly.

The man's eyes locked onto the coin in front of him before he slowly turned his head and stared down the row of shop owners to the woman at the end. His hand raised and a single damming finger pointed at her. Gallis flicked the coin in the air again and turned to walk back to the woman, not even caring if the nervous man caught the coin or scrounged for it in the dirt.

"So my dear, it seems you have lied to an official member of the royal family as well as committed treason against the throne in assisting a wanted criminal escape capture. Do you have anything to say for yourself?"

She looked up and met Gallis' gaze. Her eyes flashed with pure hatred.

"Only that I hope her highness is already so far away that you and your filth have no chance of ever getting her back. You may not realize it, but some of us know what has been happening in the shadows of that castle." She then gave Gallis a look of pure loathing that was laced with a knowing lift of her eyebrow as dropped her voice to a dull whisper. "Some of us may not be able to use magic, but it doesn't mean we can't sense it." Gallis took a step back and did a quick scan to see if anyone was close enough to hear her. The line of shopkeepers had dissolved into the surrounding crowd now that his attention wasn't on them. When he discerned only his own men stood near enough to hear he straightened himself and stared down at the woman.

"You are hereby found guilty of committing treason and assisting in the escape of a criminal wanted for attacks on his royal majesty the king. The punishment for treason is death." His voice rang out loudly and clearly across the town square. He heard the dressmaker off to the side gasp and looked over in time to see a well-dressed man hold her back from rushing to the side of who he could only guess was her sister.

Gallis turned at the sound of sliding steal as the guard who had dragged the shopkeeper pulled his sword from his side. At Gallis's nod, the guard drew up and swung, slicing the head from the woman's body in one quick motion. A scream tore from the crowd but Gallis had no interest in the dressmaker, her sister, or any of the remaining villagers in the town. He looked north towards the woods the nervous shopkeeper had indicated Arida had traveled to.

"I want a team of men scouring these woods until the princess and her elven filth are found and brought back to me." Gallis declared before mounting his nearby horse and heading back to the castle. He first though made sure to guide his horse to walk directly through the puddle of blood pooling in the dirt from the shop-keepers' body, trailing bloody footsteps through town as his reminder of obedience.

Chapter Sixteen

T heir fire was small that evening. Though Arida had found ample amounts of wood Faelyn insisted on limiting how much they fed it, so their smoke would go unseen by anyone traveling nearby. So now they sat huddled close together around their small fire nibbling on a dried fruit and coarse textured bread dinner. The horses were tied to a nearby tree nearby grazing quietly, their ears flicked at any small sound they picked up from the dark. Sometimes Arida could have sworn Faelyn's pointed ears mimicked the horses and flicked at the sound of twig snaps and leaf rustles. But then the shadow from the flames would flicker in another direction and Arida would convince herself it was just her imagination.

One thing that was becoming obvious though, was Faelyn's occasional glances to the chain around her neck. After about the fifth or sixth look, Arida couldn't take it anymore.

"Is there something you find particularly interesting about my neck?" She turned and stared him down.

"No." He said almost nonchalantly. "Not particularly. I just didn't know if you were going to bring up what happened in the throne room, or was I going to have too?" His gaze slowly lifted from the fire and met hers.

Arida stared into his intense eyes, partially shadowed from the light of the fire with his hair loose around him. She scrambled to try to explain what happened. And if she was being honest, she wasn't a hundred percent sure herself. So, the truth was easier than a lie.

"I'm not certain." She finally admitted before turning back to the fire. She lifted her hands to attempt to warm the chill running through her.

"You're not *certain*?" Faelyn asked with an accusatory tone. "You don't think it has something to do with that thing you keep hidden around your neck? And before you try to deny it, I'll remind you I have seen it before."

Arida snapped her gaze up from the flames, the memory of her naked on the bathroom floor and him rushing in to find her there flooded her mind. But there was no hint of a cocky smile or the normal emotion Arida would assume he would show on his face if he was also thinking of that. But Faelyn did have a way of hiding his emotions if he wanted that would rival even Arida's.

Almost as if he was reading her mind he chimed in again. "In the courtyard, remember? You pulled it out after I pulled you out of the arrows range? I could feel the heat radiating off of it even from where I had stood."

Arida almost felt embarrassed at her assumption as to where his thoughts had gone. Though there seemed to be a slight humorous glint to his eye now as if he had caught her assumption and turned it on her.

"It's a protection amulet." Arida finally said after thinking it over. "It's passed down through the family line to protect the heirs of the throne. It's to be kept a secret so no one tries to steal it or go for it during an attack."

Faelyn stared steadily at her, assessing if what she said was the truth or a lie. Arida kept her face smooth and expressionless hoping her answer was full enough that her omission of the other power she had recently learned it could do wouldn't be sensed. He seemed not to question her half answer because he changed the subject. "I was thinking we should head up to Parafell, we may be able to hitch a ride on a ship there and completely wipe our trail by leaving Aiden entirely."

Arida sucked in a deep breath. If they left Aiden how would her mother find them? How would she get word to her about where they ended up.

"How long will that take?"

"Well, we are about a day's ride from Moon's Bay. If we can help it, I would prefer to skirt around the port entirely just in case any palace guards stationed there have already been alerted to look for you. I was stationed there during training and when we had to do a supply run once to Parafell and it took us about five days. But that was with wagons and a dozen people. I am hoping with just the two of us we can cut it down to three days." Grabbing a stick from the woods pile Faelyn started stoking the fire causing small sparks to fly around them.

Parafell was Aiden's largest port city. There was a mural of it on one of the library walls back at home. It depicted a vast expanse of shops and homes bordering a large beach that blended to the ocean. Sailing ships littered the water that were painted with such detail that you could see the carved wooden women attached to their bows.

Arida always imagined what it would be like to see the ocean. Her parents had told her stories from their trip when her father had to go settle a trade dispute between some merchants. He had even brought her back a small vial of sand from the beach that contained a bright orange shell nestled on top that swirled and curved into the most unique shape Arida had ever seen. It sat on the mantel in her bedchamber at home. She fought the frown that tugged at the corner of her mouth and the ache that throbbed in her chest from the sadness.

They sat quietly again, the dancing flames scattering shadows around the small clearing. Occasionally Faelyn would lay another piece of wood down sending crackling sparks to skitter around them. Arida watched a few of them smolder in the dirt. The small embers pulsed orange for a few seconds before dimming to black. Eventually Arida felt her eyes getting heavy and her head start drooping. Faelyn stood and went over to the saddle bags he had dropped nearby after tying up the horses. He pulled two cylindrical rolls out of one of the canvas bags and brought them over, untying the string around each of them as he walked. He handed one over to Arida which she took and upon feeling the rough texture of wool realized it was a sleeping mat and blanket rolled together. Still standing, Faelyn grabbed the end of the roll he still held and in one quick movement snapped it out in the air in front of him and laid it gracefully on one side of the fire. Kneeling in the dirt on the opposite side Arida slowly pushed her roll out and smoothed it as much as she could, pushing gently to try to move the twigs and rocks that poked through the fabric. The ground was riddled with them so after a few swipes Arida gave up on the idea and slowly rose to her feet and started heading over to the darkened tree line.

"Where are you going?" Faelyn asked while pulling his blanket back from the bed roll.

Arida paused at the edge of the firelight. "Am I not allowed to do anything without letting you know first?" She gave him a pointed look to which he raised his hands in a 'sorry' gesture in response before she turned and headed off behind a tree she hoped was far enough away that his superior elf hearing would not hear her.

After relieving herself Arida was just starting to make her way back to their small camp when she heard horse hooves and voices. A shadow moved behind her and she froze in fear for a second before she recognized Faelyn's outline. Arida looked back towards their camp. He had been right in keeping their fire small, no sign of smoke or light could be seen through the trees. Whoever was out here with them would have to leave the road and come all the way through the dense forest and go right in the middle of their camp to find them. Faelyn's hand slid through hers and she slowly followed him back to their fire, careful to try to step exactly where his feet had been to mimic his silence. As soon as the glow of their fire touched his face, he lifted a finger to his mouth to signal it was still not safe to speak.

Arida, who moments ago was ready to curl up on her rocky banket and finally get some rest, was now too anxious to even think about sleep. She knelt on top of her blanket, those earlier pebbles digging into the soft spots on the side of her knees and watched Faelyn as he sat crouched on his heels scanning the darkness around them. Again, Arida could have sworn his ears would tilt and move when he picked up on a small sound.

Finally, after what seemed like ages of complete silence Faelyn settled into a seat on top of his blankets and looked at Arida.

"I think we are okay now." He said without whispering. An easy feeling fell back over the camp again, even the horses seemed to relax at his words. Arida also tried settling down into a more comfortable position on her bedroll. Slipping under the banket she tucked an arm under her head as a make shift pillow. She had never slept outside before; in fact, she had never slept outside of the walls of her castle. She hadn't been permitted to attend the visits her parents went on to the governors' places around the kingdom, even after her more rigorous training had begun. She was always left behind to spend her time among the other ladies of the court.

And now laying under the stars, Arida was just starting to feel how large the world really was. Shifting slightly, she glanced at Faelyn. His eyes were closed but based off the tension in his body still, he was not asleep yet. Arida quietly watched the shadows from their small fire reflect off his face and thought about her parents back at home as she slowly drifted off to sleep.

Chapter Seventeen

When Arida opened her eyes, the sun was just starting to come up, sending small pink and gold rays through the leaves of the trees. Their fire was still burning strong, Faelyn must have gotten up through the night and fed it while she slept. She glanced over to where his bed roll had been and saw only a slight indent in the grass as evidence that the elf had been there at all. She sat up quickly whipping her head back and forth. Stray strands of hair had escaped her braid during the night and stuck to her face. She brushed them out of the way as she noticed that both horses were still tied up in the same spot as the night before. She relaxed slightly as she moved her blanket off her legs and stood. Though it hadn't seemed like much, the blanket and mat partnered with the close fire had kept the cool night air at bay. Arida's breath fogged around her as she stood and turned from the bed. She had to admit the pants made moving around far easier than her skirts and dresses had been.

Faelyn was nowhere to be seen in their little clearing. Using his absence to her full advantage Arida went back into the tree line to relieve herself and straighten up her attire from sleeping. She had just finished finger brushing her hair and braiding it back again when Faelyn came from the trees to her left. He carried a small bag that had a very red tint to the bottom.

"Good, your awake." He said as he strode to the fire. He grabbed a few thicker pieces of wood from the seemingly endless pile and sat the stained bag down. He pulled some small twine out of one of his pockets and began tying the wood together.

"What's in the bag?" Arida asked, looking up from Faelyn's hands which also had a red tint to them. His gaze flicked from his project to the bag.

"Rabbits." He stated very matter of fact. "I caught them and found a stream nearby to clean them out in, figured the less trace we leave here in camp the better."

Arida glanced at the bag again, wondering if maybe he also chose to butcher them out of her sight as a kindness to her as well. She wasn't sure what she would have thought if she had woken to him gutting and skinning the rabbits in front of her. Which was ironic that she had already watched him kill men several times and she was never left conflicted from that. But on the other hand, it's not like these rabbits had tried to kidnap and or kill her.

Faelyn's hands made quick work of his little project, binding the sticks together and soon he was setting it up over the fire. He then pulled strips of meat out of the bag and threaded them on the long stick that was just out of reach of the flames. Every now and again he would spin the stick to cook a different side of his catch. The aroma of the cooking meat had Arida's mouth watering and stomach growling. The small meal the night before had been enough to fill her stomach at the time.

But now the food was long gone and her stomach was rumbling and twisting in hunger.

Thankfully the strips of meat did not take all that long to cook and Faelyn soon pulled pieces off and handed them over to her. The meat was hot and greasy. Arida had not eaten with her fingers since she was a small child. So, it was a novel feeling when she bit into the meat and could feel the juice dribble down her fingers and hand. She had eaten rabbit before, but always seasoned and formally served. But even though it was a little bland, Arida had to admit the meat was rather tasty. The fire helped by adding a smokiness to it.

They ate in silence until all the rabbit was gone. Faelyn grabbed one of their water skins and took a swig before dumping a little over his hands to rinse the sheen of grease off. He then handed the bottle over and Arida gladly took it and mirrored what he had done.

"When did you want to leave?" Arida asked as Faelyn stowed the water canteen away.

Faelyn opened his mouth to answer, but before he could speak a word the sound of something large crashing through the trees ripped apart their quiet morning. Faelyn jumped to his feet so fast he was a blur of red hair. A look of panicked confusion flashed across his face a second before he reached down and grabbed Arida by the wrist yanking her up into a standing position. Before she could even get her feet underneath her Faelyn was pulling her across the clearing and throwing her up onto the back of her horse. Grabbing his own reins he swung himself into the saddle somehow simultaneously untying the horses with a quick tug at the knot securing that had secured them to the sapling.

Just as Faelyn hit his saddle a horse with an armored rider burst through the other side of the clearing. He paused for a moment at the sight of them. He wore the black colors of Gallis's personal guard. He made a whistled alert and as soon as another guard breached their clearing Faelyn yelled at Arida and took off into the woods at full speed. Arida's horse, now spooked followed swiftly running on the heels of its companions. How had Faelyn not heard them coming? Arida wondered as branches and leaves whipped across her face stinging her skin. She tucked as low to her horse as she could. She glanced back and was shocked to see the guards still close behind, but the only sound she could hear was the pounding of her own horses' hooves, and those of Faelyn's ahead of her. The hooves of the soldiers' horses bounded silently against the hard ground. But there was no warmth around Arida's neck, so it would seem whatever magic had been used to silence their footsteps was not being done so by an active Spellborn. Arida turned back forward, hoping they could outrun the group behind them. How Faelyn knew where they were or where they were headed, she didn't know. Luckily her horse seemed to sense the urgency and stayed close behind her lead, following every sharp turn and straight away. But it seemed no matter how fast they went the guards behind them stayed just as close.

Arida turned around again to see if she could catch sight of them but the speed the world was whipping by threatened to make her sick, so she turned back around and tucked her face low again.

Arida was once again glad in Faelyn's choice of horses. They maintained their run through the forest without pause or needing to be signaled along. Her horse was breathing hard, puffing small clouds in the chilled air. Arida was beginning to miss the comfortability of her saddle from home. This one was thin and hard and was really starting to make her sore. Arida shifted about trying to find a spot that was maybe more comfortable. She shifted her hip to the left and just after her body followed an arrow whizzed through the air where her head had just been. The arrow zipped past her horse's ear and lodge into a tree nearby.

"Watch your back!" Arida yelled as another arrow shot by her. This one barely missing the rear haunch of Faelyn's horse.

Faelyn swore as he swung his leg around and turned in his saddle, pulling something out of one of the saddle bags as he did. Arida watched from between her horses' ears as he pulled back the instrument in his hand and released. A small ball shaped item shot out of it and zipped over Arida's head. Without turning around

Arida heard a loud metallic ting sound followed by a loud thud which Arida could only guess was the ball hitting one of the guards' helmets and him falling from his horse.

Arida risked another peak back and saw the fallen soldier had served as reminder to the others that one of their own traveled with her. And his skillset was much more advanced it would seem as they had slowed enough to still be able to follow but to hopefully stay out of range of Faelyn's small but effective weapon.

"We are close to Moon's Bay!" Faelyn shouted, pulling his what Arida now recognized as a slingshot back again. "If we can make it there, we might be able to find a place to lay low!"

"I thought you said we couldn't go there." Arida yelled back. Another ting and thud rang out again. She also was shocked at the distance they had covered. But then again when Faelyn originally said a day's ride, he wasn't expecting to be traveling at the break neck speed they had been.

"I said I would prefer not to. But at this point it will be the easiest place to lose these guys." He let loose another small ball, another ting, another thud.

The horses breathing was becoming increasingly louder, more strained. Arida began to worry what would happen if they didn't make it to Moon's Bay. Faelyn had taken out enough of the guards with his slingshot that the arrows had stopped and they seemed to be following at a greater distance than before.

Just as Arida thought the horses were going to have to stop for fear of them dropping dead of exhaustion, she spied a large structure emerging from the woods. It was a large brick wall, similar to the one she would see on her rides near the edge of the palace grounds and suddenly her chest swelled with hope.

"It's the outer guard wall of Moon's Bay!" Faelyn yelled over his shoulder. He pulled his horse to the right and began following the curve of the wall.

The terrain around them had been for the most part the same. Same tall oak trees, shrubs and various leafy plants. A few pine trees were sprinkled in as well but nothing out of the ordinary. But as they rode against the wall Arida began to notice the forest changing around them. Vines were beginning to creep in against the bricks of the wall. The grass was becoming a darker shade of green and the plants had a more menacing look to them. Thorns and spines were growing out of leaves and shrubs that before had looked completely harmless. Just as Arida opened her mouth to ask Faelyn about what she noticed she felt the amulet begin to warm against her chest. Arida whipped her head back and forth to try to find the source of power it was sensing but saw nothing. She was scanning the trees and was so focused on looking for the cause of the amulets reaction that she didn't see the vine that snaked out in front of her horse seemingly on its own. It caught the horse's front ankle enough to make her trip forward launching Arida right out of her saddle.

Arida had the weightless sensation of flying through the air for about three seconds before she made contact with the earth. She luckily had the forethought of tucking herself into a ball before she hit, but the impact caused a sharp pain to radiate from her right shoulder and down her spine causing the air to whoosh out of her lungs.

Arida laid there in the grass dazed for a few moments. Gasping like a fish on land trying to get air back into her chest. The necklace's heat grew in intensity and Arida's hand grabbed at the front of her shirt trying to pull it away from her skin. Finally, she caught a breath back into her and rolled to her side. Her shoulder ached already and her back tingled with angry nerves, but everything still seemed to move as it should.

She looked around trying to find her horse or Faelyn, but saw no one. Her fall had been silent, Arida hadn't let a peep out from the moment she left her saddle to when she made impact. But Faelyn's hearing should have picked up on the sound of the disruption of her horse's gait, and her subsequent fall. Hopefully he was trying to rein his horse around and come back for her.

Slowly Arida pulled herself to her knees. She cradled her shoulder with her opposite hand wincing as the movement made it throb. As she glanced around searching for her horse or Faelyn the familiar sound of horse hooves thumped against the ground, but from the wrong direction.

Whatever spell that had been used to silence their steps had either worn off or had been broken. Gallis's men came riding up on her fast. There were only three of them now so they quickly moved around her, forming a triangle as they came to a stop and looked down on her. Arida could feel her stomach drop to the ground as she realized she had absolutely zero way of stopping these men from taking her. She released her hold on the necklace allowing it to slip back into its hiding place. The metal scorching her skin the whole way down.

One began to dismount his horse. The amulet around her neck was burning hot, and her pulse was roaring in her ears as she watched the man step down. His armor clanked against itself as he moved. More horse hooves thumped, but from which direction Arida couldn't say. She sat there kneeling before them, clutching her arm to her chest feeling like a field mouse cornered by a barn cat. And the heat building on her chest now had grown so strong it felt like it was a part of her, coming from deep inside of her.

And as the soldier made another step toward her, the horse hooves thundered closer as well. The heat becoming too much to be contained any longer. With the sound of a sword being unsheathed by the man in front of her Arida released a scream as heat and power surged from her. Bright white light flooded out into the forest. The amulet like a living flame sitting on her skin, trying to burn its way out from under her clothes. She lost all sense of anything around her. She could no longer see the guards or their horses. She could hear nothing from the forest around her. Nothing but her own scream that still rang in her ears as the overwhelming sense of power flooded over her.

But just as quickly as the power surged to her it began to die down. And as it lagged, so did her energy. The white light ceased and Arida collapsed to the forest floor.

Chapter Eighteen

The world came back in a blurry, tilted haze. A loud ringing sounded through Arida's ears and as her head shifted to the side the forest spun around her. She could make out the metallic glean of armored feet sticking out from the brush just to her right. That meant one guard was handled, but what of the others?

She shifted on her back trying to slide her arms up her side to brace into a sitting position. The world flashed white and the ringing doubled in volume as her muscles tensed to support her weight. Slowly though her senses began to clear and straighten as she took in the forest around her.

Plants were swept down as if a large wind had raced through and forced them to bow. She noticed again the soldiers' feet lying beside her. Attached to them was a man who laid unmoving and from the way his lower half was twisted in a different direction from his upper it was clear he would stay that way. Her gaze slowly drifted around, past the dead man. The twisting plants and odd vines she had seen while riding through had disappeared. Nothing but some thorn tipped leaves scattered on the ground remained.

Movement to her left caught Arida's attention. Faelyn dodged around a nearby tree that sported some freshly snapped branches dangling limply and came swiftly towards her. His hair was disheveled and he had a panicked expression on his face as he sank to his knees in front of her. Arida watched his mouth move for a few seconds before it stopped and pressed into a hard line. Her dazed, blank expression must have told him enough that she was not comprehending what he was trying to say because he stopped trying to speak and instead just grabbed her by the upper arms and pulled her up to stand with him. Her knees were wobbly, but they held. The rest of the small clearing looked like it faired the same as the part she could see from her position in the grass. The remaining two soldiers laid not far off and were in a similar askew positions as the first. Thrown from their horses that were now nowhere to be seen, the force of the landing seemed to have resulted in their chest armor to have been crushed inward. But as to the twisted nature of their arms and legs Arida couldn't quite figure out what could have caused that. Faelyn tugged on her arm and Arida was still so stunned from what had just unfolded, she followed his tugs unquestioningly as he pulled her into the tree. They ducked under branches and zig zagged through the forest. As her blood began pumping more with the exertion of stumbling quickly behind the elf, Arida's vision steadied itself finally back to normal and her hearing was slowly coming back.

As they turned around a large tree Arida spotted Faelyn's horse standing in a small clearing. She was restless, pacing back and forth. The mare was untied and Faelyn had used his exceptional sense of hearing to lead them to her. The elf put his hand on the horse's neck and stroked her mane, comforting the animal. Arida wasn't sure where her mare had gone off to after being spooked. She clearly was not with her companion.

The elf turned and glanced at Arida. "So, you want to tell me what that was back there?" He continued to comfort the horse until he was able to reach around and grab the reins from where they draped on the ground.

"I'm not sure." Arida muttered leaning up against the nearest tree. Her body suddenly feeling very heavy.

"You're not sure? You almost blew everything around you to smithereens and you're not sure?" Faelyn turned to face her with an incredulous look on his face. "The men back there, they looked just like the ones in the throne room."

"I know." Arida whispered, resisting the urge to grab the amulet "But I don't know what it was. I was just sitting there and they were circling me one minute and the next..." She looked up and stared at Faelyn. He met her gaze and said nothing, his eyes roamed her face, perhaps looking for a sign she was being untruthful. "The amulet clearly has a strong reaction when it senses I'm in trouble. But I have no idea how to control it."

Faelyn's gaze flickered to her chest for a moment as if he could see it through her clothes. "I've never heard of an object, even a magical one having free will to cause that kind of damage. There has to be more to it, some kind of direction it gets from you..." He trailed off staring at her some more. Was he accusing her of being spell-born? Arida wondered matching the elf's stare with a cold one of her own.

"If it is" she replied back through clenched teeth "It's unknown. I haven't the slightest idea about how the events in the throne room and back there in the forest took place." The pair stood there staring at each other until Faelyn seemed to accept the answer, she had given him and shrugged. "We seem to only get more questions and less answers when it comes to that thing." At that he turned and pulled himself into the saddle of their lone horse. He then twisted to angle his body angled towards her with an outstretched an arm, though he didn't meet her gaze. "We need to keep moving." Was all he said, clearly done now with conversations about the strange happenings and magical accusations.

Arida glanced around them for a moment, hoping her mare would walk through the trees any second and save her from having to ride in front of the elf.

"She's some distance from here, we will have to ride to find her again." Faelyn said, arm still out waiting.

Reluctantly Arida walked forward and grasped Faelyn's forearm. Without a second thought he easily pulled her up into the front section of the saddle. She grabbed the back of her riding cape and tucked it between them to keep it from tangling in the horses' front legs, and also to create some distance between his body and her own. If he realized her second motive, he didn't show it as he loosely held the reins in front of them and tapped the horse into a trot. His height easily allowed him to see over her head and patrol their surroundings.

They headed away from the wall they had before followed closely. Faelyn said he had heard her horse run deep into the woods just before Arida had exploded the world around them. They were now following a trail of small broken twigs and faint hoof prints only elven eyes could track.

They paused for a small lunch after a few hours and Arida was glad to get down and get some distance between her and the elf, the constant jostling and close contact was growing increasingly uncomfortable. She had tried to keep her posture as rigid as possible to prevent as little touching as possible, and thanks to her mother's rigorous etiquette training she had been able to hold it for the first few hours of their ride without a problem. But now that she was free from the position, she found herself stretching against the trunk of a tree, trying to relieve the tension in the muscles along her spine and deep in her core. She could have sworn she saw the elf smirk for a moment at her discomfort before he turned and rummaged through his saddle bags for food.

They spilt a small portion of nuts and dried fruit, Arida realized that outside of their personal comfort they were put in a bad position if they were unable to find her horse simply because of the saddle bags full of food and gear they would lose with her. Not to mention the bed rolls and blankets still on the ground at this morning's camp they had already lost.

Luckily the pouch of coin left from her mother Faelyn had tucked into one of the pockets near his chest so it had not been lost. Quietly they ate, and after she popped the last dried apple piece in her mouth, Arida used the opportunity off the horse to walk around and stretch her legs. Her body was sore from more than just the horse riding. The heaviness she had felt in the clearing had lessoned a little bit but it felt like even her bones were heavier inside her body. The way the amulet had worked in the clearing confused her. How did it know she was in trouble? Was it somehow connected to her through her ancestors? Her mother had always said it was her responsibility now, and that it would keep her safe. But how? Unlike Faelyn, Arida did not believe that she herself was affecting the way it behaved. Spellborns were magical with or without magical objects, and she clearly did not have powers. There was however another kind of heaviness that weighed upon her that was not so easily stretched out and that was the knowledge that she had definitely killed those men back near the wall. The ones in the throne room she assumed hadn't made it, but she hadn't stuck around long enough to check. But the men in the clearing, they were definitely dead.

She was mulling over everything that had happened over. The information she had been taught about the amulet; the feelings she had knowing she had taken lives now. All the while she was weaving in and out of the trees in small circles, back and forth.

"Can you stop that already? Your worrying is making the horse uneasy." Faelyn said gruffly, breaking her concentration. He was leaning against a tree, a small twig tucked between his teeth, his hands shoved in the front pockets of his pants. He was the picture of ease, as if he was just hanging out in the woods on any regular day. He didn't seem to have any qualms over what had happened earlier. Arida stopped and straightened. Her face the mask she had been taught to wear, no matter what she was feeling on the inside she couldn't let it show.

"I am not worrying, I am thinking." Arida replied coolly.

"Ah, my mistake." Faelyn straightened and moved back to the horse. "I just assumed since you seemed to be carving out quite the path in between those trees."

Arida just glared and stalked forward fighting the urge to look at the ground. "Are we going to continue to find my horse now?"

"No." Faelyn said, plucking the twig out of his mouth and tossing it to the ground before checking the clasps on the saddle bags.

"What do you mean, no?" Arida put her hands on her hips and stared at the back of his head.

"I mean we have wasted enough time trying to track that horse down and for all we know she could be halfway back to Clarea by now. The way I see it, we would be better off heading back to Moon's Bay, find a place to stay low for the night and get more supplies in the morning." Faelyn pulled himself back into the saddle and reached back down for Arida like he had earlier.

"I thought it was too dangerous for us to go to Moons Bay, what if someone recognizes us? We aren't being chased down now; can't we go back to our original plan?" Arida kept her hands on her hips and stared him down from the ground.

"Well, with only half the supplies now, I don't think we can make it to another town with what we have. And clearly, I underestimated how motivated Gallis is to get you back. Plus with our new little development of whatever that was back there I think we could use a night to rethink and replan. And I would prefer to do so with a warm meal I didn't have to prepare and four solid walls around us."

He was right of course, no matter how much that irritated her. So Arida reached up and allowed the elf to once again pull her into the saddle in front of him. After she had positioned herself comfortably with her cloak once again tucked in close between them Faelyn tugged the reins and they began a slow trot back to the wall.

Chapter Nineteen

Faelyn directed the horse back to the outer wall of Moon's Bay, and then used it as a guide to bring them to front gates. He skillfully avoided all the roads and paths leading to the entrance therefor also avoiding any other travelers who may have already been instructed to look out for the pair by any passing palace guards.

Arida had noted that the forest had maintained the same normal plant life near the section of the wall they came out to as any other part of the forest. No oddities in the appearance or behaviors like it had before they were cornered. When Arida voiced her observation, she felt Faelyn tense behind her.

"Magic has been gone for a long time, but there are still odd pockets in the realm where its influence was strong and the effects still linger."

"How can it linger and be gone? I've never heard of these pockets before." Arida half turned in the saddle, trying to assess the elf's face.

"There aren't many, and they are avoided in conversation as much as they should be avoided in life. They are not true magic, at least in the sense of what magic used to be. It's said these are remnants from the days of Koening, scraps left over from events that imprinted it into the land." Faelyn shifted the reins urging the horse to continue following the curve of the wall.

Arida found it odd that he was so knowledgeable about the magic that was still active in the world.

"Is this something the elves talk about?" Arida asked, trying to keep her voice level and not accusatory. If the elves were tracking magical remnants, what else could they be up to? They were known followers of the ancient sorcerer and since they had hidden away in their forests at the edge of Aiden very little was known about the goings on of them as a people.

"Not just the elves." Faelyn said gruffly "We have only made it a few miles outside of your palace where you've experienced very little of the kingdom around you. But you'll see as we travel there's more things to learn about the realm you rule than what your mother has taught you. And not every place we go will look like the cared for and groomed lawns and forests around your castle."

Arida bristled at the inference of her mother hiding from her what her kingdom was like. But it was true, she had never seen for herself the area outside of her palace walls. But Arida was not as naïve about magic as the elf assumed.

Her mother and her had discussed magic numerous times in her private lessons. It had been mixed in with her family's early history. Before her ancestor Collete's battle with Koening, the palace had enlisted some of the most powerful magic users in history. A blend of great warriors and healers kept the kingdom flourish-ing. But with the history there came the strongest of warnings to never share the information with anyone. Since her mother's revelation that Collete herself had been a magic user Arida could see why her mother didn't want any information about the inner workings of their families past with magic discussed. Especially since it wouldn't take much for the history to get contorted through the rumor mill and misspoke to make people think their current rulers were trying to access magic rather than irradicate those who were. Though the memory of Gallis' wind in the throne room was enough to send a chill racing down Arida's spine.

She clutched her cloak a little tighter around her as they passed under an archway of trees. The wall curved sharply and as the horse rounded the corner, they saw the dirt road come back into view. It led towards the wall where a set of small guard towers with a large wooden door between them. Two men stood inside little alcoves carved out of the base of each tower.

Faelyn slowed the horses and used his closeness to Arida to whisper.

"I will do all the talking. Try to keep your head down, you never know which guards used to be stationed at the palace and were reassigned to work down here. Some may know your face."

Arida glanced through the trees towards the guards. "Okay." She whispered back and grabbed the edge of her hood, pulling it up to hide herself as much as possible.

Faelyn turned the horse and back tracked through some thick brush and brought them back to the road just out of view from the main gate.

"Why?" Arida started before Faelyn cut in.

"Emerging like ghosts from the forest would look suspicious and raise more questions. Normal travelers use the road"

Arida was surprised how exposed she felt out of the cover of the forest when the guards came back into view. She almost wished she had ridden behind Faelyn so that his body would have covered her more from view. They moved out from their stations in the shadows as the single horse approached.

"We wish to gain entry for the night." Faelyn announced as he reined the horse to a stop. Arida kept her face down as the guards assessed them. Hoping they had never served up at the palace and recognized her. They appeared more interested in Faelyn than her though.

"And what exactly are your plans for the night?" The guard on the left asked in a tone that could only be described as a sneer. His gaze then raked over Arida.

"We plan to find a place to stay and eat a decent meal before carrying on to our next destination." Faelyn replied coolly, acting as if he hadn't picked up the tone used towards him.

"And what is your relationship with the lady you travel with?" The guard on the right questioned.

"She's my half-sister." Faelyn replied smoothly and without hesitation. "We share a father but have different mothers. We are to meet up with him and his fishing vessel in Port Lenore in less than a week. We have traveled a long way and wish to spend a night in real beds and eat a hot meal before we continue on our way."

"Is that true miss?" The guard with the sneer asked. His eyes moved up and down Arida's frame.

"Aye." Is all Arida replied trying to keep as much of her face tucked under her hood as possible.

The guards looked at each other before moving to the gate behind them. Each grabbed a handle and pulled, making an opening just wide enough for them to pass through.

"We thank you." Faelyn said and directed the horse on. They received only looks of disgust as they passed.

Arida could feel their stares on her back until the thud of the gates shut behind them

Chapter Twenty

Moon's Bay was called such because of the crescent shape the city was built in around the cove. The water here was shallow, so only small vessels were docked in the bay itself. The city was vast compared to Clarea. Homes were built close to the wall and near one another stair stepping down in rows towards the water. Shops and hotels filtered down until the water's edge where a brick retaining wall was constructed to keep large waves from storms out of the streets and town. People milled around the main road with bags and belongings, none paying the travelers any mind. Guards were stationed every so often at various points in the city patrolling the wall, the stores, the bay. All were wearing the traditional burgundy colored garb of royal guards; Gallis's colors were nowhere in sight.

"There's an inn nearby where we may be able to stay. It has an attached stable we can keep the horse in for the night as well." Faelyn spoke quietly into Arida's ear. She simply nodded in reply. Her eyes had been scanning the town and the people that walked about but her gaze shifted and suddenly locked on the shimmering water of the bay.

Never before had she seen such a grand expanse of water, it went on and on into the horizon before it blended into the sky. The light blue shimmered and flashed the gold tones of the sun. It was almost blinding. It reminded Arida of the gemstones from her mother's favorite necklace, they were light blue and shimmery and as a child she always imagined that they had captured a piece of the sea and held it forever inside the cool casing of stone. A small smile tugged at her lips from the memory, but she quickly smothered it. Arida had always imagined what the sea looked like. She had seen it in paintings around the castle but they did nothing to capture the beauty and movements of the water. Nor could they have prepared her for the salty tang it gave to the air the closer they got to it. The loud voices of the fishermen hauling their days catch onto the dock blended with the soft crashing of the waves and the subtle creaking the tie up boats made as they gently bobbed. The sights, sounds, and smells were everything Arida had imagined when she dreamt of seeing the sea. Again, she fought back a smile.

If Faelyn had seen it, he made no comment. He just slowly guided the horse away from the water and towards the inn, though Arida noted his hands tightened a fraction on the reins and their horse walked a tad slower allowing Arida to soak up the sight a moment longer.

The inn was a moderate sized building with three floors and a thatched roof that had a slight green tint from the continuous spray of the sea. It did indeed have a small stable near the back, Faelyn brought the horse around and helped Arida dismount. A stable boy who couldn't have been older than fourteen came jogging out to meet them. Faelyn handed him a few coins after removing the saddle bags and threw them over his own shoulder.

"We are only staying the night, see to it the horse is fed and watered. And if you happen to know where we can get a second horse, I'll throw in another copper piece."

The boy tucked the coins into his pocket and nodded eagerly before grabbing the reins and leading the horse into its room for the night.

Faelyn turned and motioned for Arida to follow him.

The inside of the inn was poorly lit and not what Arida would have called overly clean. A small counter sat on the right side of the great room and a tavern bar sat at the back, a small wooden staircase sat just to the left of the door. Scattered throughout the room was a collection of mismatched wooden tables and chairs, many of whom were occupied by men just as mismatched as the furniture.

Sailors, travelers and townspeople all were posted up in the chairs. All with drinks, many with food.

"Come on, let's go see if they have room." Faelyn started towards the small counter that had a man standing behind it. He straightened up as he saw the pair near.

He was a portly man, and far shorter than herself. He was almost completely bald and was built like one of the pigs Arida would see in the barns in the palace.

"We are looking for lodgings for the night." Faelyn said as soon as he reached the counter.

"Aye" The man said eyeing them closely. His eyes paused when he noticed the points of Faelyn's ears. "One room or two?" His gaze then flicked to Arida, raking over her up and down. He was unable to see her ears under her hood she still had raised, but that didn't seem to be his reason for looking.

"One." Faelyn said and Arida stiffened. The innkeeper turned to fish a key out of one of the small cubbies that lined the wall behind him.

"One?" She all but growled under her breath as she glared up at the elf.

Without meeting her look he whispered back so low she doubted the man in front of them heard "Yes, one. Do you really think I am going to leave you all alone in a place like *this*? Look around, do you see a single woman in here?"

Arida swept the room again and noticed he was correct. She was the only female in the room. And it appeared several of the men in their chairs had noticed this as well. Their gazes were fixed on her and most didn't seem ashamed they had been caught looking. Arida clenched her teeth and decided she would continue this conversation later.

The innkeeper handed over a key with one hand and accepted the coins in the other. A large blue tag hung from the end of the key with a white number sixteen painted on it. The man looked at Arida again and smiled at her in a way that made her skin crawl. She turned and kept a little closer to Faelyn's shoulder as he headed to the staircase.

The stairs creaked as they ascended to the second floor. Faelyn turned and walked down the hall, stopping when he came to the door that matched the key's number tag. He held the door open and gestured for Arida to go in. She ducked by him and found herself in a small room just as dim as the main one downstairs. A bed sat against the far wall and a nightstand with a single candle lamp sat beside it. A pair of chairs sat under the lone window. Thin curtains hung limply from a curtain rod Arida would almost swear used to be a broom handle, now cut short.

The bed was big enough for two but the thought of sharing a bed with not only a male but a male who had already seen her naked once made her cross her arms tightly around her chest and stand in the middle of the room staring at it.

"The doors lock you know." She said finally breaking the silence. Faelyn had stuck the saddle bags on top of one of the chairs and had begun silently digging through them. "I don't see why I couldn't have just stayed in my own room. You've protected me from outside a locked door before."

"Yes." Faelyn said finally righting himself. "But that was in a palace, surrounded by other guards. And not in a cagey inn filled with men who looked like they had won a prize the moment you walked in."

Arida squeezed her arms tighter around her.

"Trust me, I want to share a bed with you just as much as you want to share one with me."

She turned and faced him, giving him an incredulous look.

"You talk in your sleep and on occasion snore."

Arida threw her arms down, her hands balled into fists. "I do not snore!"

Faelyn just chuckled and went back to doing his inventory on their gear.

"And how would you know anyway? You guarded from outside my bedchamber."

Without turning from what he was doing he lifted one hand and tapped the tip of his ear. "Elf, remember? It's not all that difficult to hear through walls, even stone ones."

"I don't snore." Arida grumbled again and sat on the edge of the bed. But she did wonder at what he might have heard her say in her sleep. She knew she talked in her sleep sometimes. Her mother said Arida had since she was a toddler, always mumbling out loud whatever was happening in her dreams. She toyed with that thought in her head until she was interrupted by the loud sound of her stomach rumbling.

"I'm starving, when can we go down and get something to eat?"

Faelyn peered out the curtains. "We could go now, I wanted to give the early dinner crowd a chance to clear out. But I really don't want to wait too long and the late nighters show up. That's a group of men I could do without you meeting."

Arida nodded in quick agreement and rose. She too would like to miss that particular crowd.

Together they walked out of the room, Faelyn stopping to lock the door before they headed down to find food and hopefully a quiet table away from others.

Chapter Twenty One

Faelyn had been good at his timing. A lot more tables were empty now than there had been when they had gone upstairs. The innkeeper was still behind his counter and gave Arida another one of his filthy smiles. She turned quickly and hurried after the elf. He put her at a small table away from the remainder of the patrons before going up to the bar to order their food. A female with an apron on was over at another table now, but she appeared more interested in dancing her fingers around the rim of the ale goblet that was sitting on the table in front of a large man dressed like a sailor than taking anyone's order.

Arida watched as the man that was tending bar finally took Faelyn's order after ignoring him for several minutes. Choosing to wipe down the same glass for several moments and look up to check if anyone else needed any help rather than acknowledge Faelyn. Though the elf didn't show it Arida thought how that must have bothered him. But he spoke calmly and politely to the barkeep and then leaned up against the counter to wait as the man went through a swinging door, presumably to the kitchen.

Arida glanced around at the others in the room. The men were older, many dressed like sailors, some had the worn clothes of travelers. All of the others Arida assumed must have been townspeople who just liked to hang around for the drinks and the conversation.

They indeed all had a large pitcher of ale in front of them and full glasses in each hand. It had clearly not been their first pitcher either as they were speaking very loud and boisterous. Their voices echoed through the large room, and Arida overheard a variety of conversations ranging from how many women they had to keep them company and who had mouthed off to the wrong guard and found himself in the local jail. But slowly those morphed into talks about days out at sea and travels they had taken.

After a few minutes Faelyn came walking over with two trays. He set one down in front of her and took his to the chair opposite hers. The trays each had identical cups of wine, a small roll and a steaming plate of roast meat and vegetables.

"The cook didn't say what kind of meat it is, but if I had to guess I would say its venison from the smell of it." Faelyn said as he picked up his fork and knife and began cutting away pieces of the meat. Arida couldn't care if it was beef, venison or whatever mystery meat the cook had conjured up, she was so glad to have something hot in her belly. She too was quickly carving away pieces of the meat and shoving it into her mouth.

The meat was tough and flavorless and the vegetables were overcooked and turned to mush when she tried to spear them with her fork but Arida ate every piece of it. She glanced up and saw Faelyn had already cleared his plate and was now leaning back in his chair with his roll in one hand and his glass of wine in the other. They had spent the last few meals eating nothing but cold dry fruit and cheese aside from the small rabbit they had shared so they both ate their meal quickly. When Arida too was sitting back and enjoying her cup of wine she for the first time in days felt warm and full.

The men from across the bar voices raised again. In her haste to eat Arida hadn't noticed a few more tables fill in. Sailors who were in port for the night had struck up conversation with the earlier men and they were now talking boisterously, their deep voices echoing easily in the small dining space.

"I'm telling you it was a creature from lore." One of the sailors proclaimed slamming his mug on the table. Arida glanced to Faelyn and saw his attention was already on the group.

"It came out of the deep and went right for the lead ship in the fleet. The *Rose* didn't even stand a chance. The beast had tentacles taller than the mast, and within minutes had the ship sunk and men screaming." The sailor shook his head and took a long drink from his mug.

"That's impossible." One of the older men sitting just a table over said. "Beasts like that are just myths, they disappeared from the world just like everything else that was sustained by magic." A few men grumbled in agreement.

"I'm not the only one who's seen creatures such as this. There's whispers and stories at other ports of strange things that are happening out in the open water." The sailors' eyes had a haunted look that made Arida believe the horrors he had seen to be true.

Other sailors started nodding along, agreeing with the rumors they had heard. Arida glanced at Faelyn who simply shrugged at her.

Another man in worn traveler clothes piped in "There's all kinds of odd goings on in the kingdom. I've heard it from my sister who lives in Clarea that the princess was kidnapped by a rogue guard after an attack on the kings and her uncle has been searching the whole of Aiden for her. He even went so far as to kill a shopkeeper who was conspiring to hide the princess's whereabouts from him. Did it right the in the square for all to see."

Arida felt her body go rigid. She tried to freeze her face in an uncaring expression. Could it be? The face of the shopkeeper flashed in her mind. The woman who had known who she was and had promised to keep her secret, died for doing as she promised.

"Perhaps we should finish our wine upstairs." Faelyn whispered. Arida turned and saw him studying her face.

"Perhaps that's best." Arida agreed. And grabbed her glass and quietly stood from her chair. The men were still discussing the various other rumors they had heard about their missing princess as Faelyn led her back upstairs. Just before she hit the top step Arida heard a man's voice follow her up the stairs.

"Goodnight, lady."

Arida turned and looked behind her in time to see the Inn keeper slyly wave and wink before he walked up to the bar. She turned and quickly took the last few stairs. Faelyn had an odd expression on his face when she met him at the door. She couldn't quite tell what it was, a mixture of anger and laughter.

"What's with you?" She asked going past him into the room.

"Nothing at all. I just can't decide if I find it funny or irritating the amount of attention our charming inn keeper is giving you."

"You find his creepy behavior funny?" Arida whipped around and glared at him. The wine in her cup sloshed slightly onto the floor.

"No, I find your reaction funny." Faelyn locked the door behind him and after setting his own cup down on the chair by his bags he gestured for her to move to the side, away from the center of the room she was standing in.

Arida shifted to the direction he indicated, confused as to what he was about to do. "And what about my reaction is so funny to you?"

Faelyn looked her straight in the eye with one of his smug grins. "I find it so funny because your reactions make it obvious you have no idea how to respond to the opposite sex when they make a pass at you. You get all confused and red. Which to see on your face is hilarious." Arida shot him a dirty look. "I would find it funnier though if it was someone who hasn't made it so clear that he has zero plan to leave you alone while we are here."

At that Faelyn turned and grabbed the metal headboard of the bed and pulled. The size and entire metal framework of the bed made it have to weigh several hundred pounds, but Faelyn made it look like it was little more than one of the bed rolls they had been sleeping on the past few nights as he pulled the bed across the floor and shoved it against the door. The old iron protested as it was forced to shift.

"There" he said picking his wine glass back up and sitting down onto one of the chairs "that should keep out even those with a key."

Arida stared at the bed now pushed securely against the door and fought off a shiver. She hadn't even thought about the creepy front desk man possibly having a spare key to the rooms. Let alone doing something to keep him from being able to use it. She looked back at the elf leaning casually in the old chair and was bringing his wine back to his wine tinted lips. He smiled at her before taking a sip.

"Trained bodyguard, remember?" He chuckled before resting his cup back on his leg. "And that is also why one room."

Arida relaxed her face from her astounded expression and settled onto the bed, very aware that the metal headboard gently bumped the door as she did. She pulled her legs up to her chest and wrapped her arms around them, careful not to slosh any of her wine on the sheets.

"So, what's our plan now?" Arida asked, hesitant to raise her voice above a whisper for fear of any prying ears that may be listening. Especially any that were pointed.

"Well, it's only a matter of time before the bodies of those men are discovered outside the wall. And news will travel back to your uncle fast about what befell them. So, we can't stay here longer than tonight." Faelyn paused and swirled his wine thinking before he spoke again. I think our best bet is still to find a ship that can take us from here. I just worry that traveling the coast line on a small vessel is a bad idea. There are not enough places to hide if Gallis and his men catch up to us again, and too many other travelers going the same way, someone eventually would recognize you and turn us in."

Faelyn paused for a moment, Arida was just about to ask him to go on when she heard the pounding of footsteps coming down the hall. She bit her tongue and waited. A man said something muffled and a woman laughed loudly, their footsteps traveling past their door. When the thud of another door closed down the hall Faelyn continued.

"I think our best bet is to ride south to the next port then cut inland, follow the banks of the Corvack river to one of the bigger coastal villages that were made where it empties back out to the eastern sea. We can find bigger ships there and pick our destination once we have our options."

Arida thought about it for a moment and then remembered the biggest obstacle that they would have to face if they traveled along the Corvack.

"What about the Mathwich Mountains? The river travels straight through them and It's already cold here, I don't even want to think about how cold it would be traveling in the shadow of the Twin Peaks." Arida could almost feel the frost nipping at her finger tips from just the thought of it. The Mathwich Mountains were somewhere Arida had never seen but her father had traveled there once when she was about six. A small village near the base of the Eastern Twin had called for aid in arming themselves better against a clan of mountain men that had been plaguing them. Her father had gone with a small army and wagons of supplies. He had been gone for nearly a month before he returned. His nose had gone so red and chapped from the continuous cold that Arida had been afraid it would fall of his face. She had been young and her mother had tried to explain to her over and over again how that wouldn't happen. What the Queen hadn't known was that the night before the king had sat on the edge of Arida's bed and told her some of his stories from his trip and how several men had lost toes from the cold.

"Aye," he had said while tucking her blankets snug around her. "A few of the men came back to the tents one evening complaining of foot pain. And wouldn't you believe it, when they took their boots of some of their toes had just fallen right off...."

It was weeks before Arida could look at any of the guards around the castle and not wonder if they had all their toes or not.

Faelyn shifted in his seat drawing Arida's attention back to the present.

"Well, there's a path we could take that will lead us around the base of them. We won't avoid them entirely but we shouldn't have to actually travel through them."

Arida nodded, it sounded like a better plan than what she could have come up with.

"I say we head out first thing in the morning. Refill the supplies we lost with your horse and head straight out. Once we get a few hours from here it should be safe enough to travel on the road again if we stay vigilant. That will make it easier for us to gain more distance from the palace and hopefully the reach of your uncle. We can check the ports as we go, who knows maybe we get lucky and find a ship dropping cargo that we can catch and avoid the mountains all together." Faelyn looked into his cup and downed the remaining wine he had left.

"We should probably get some sleep now. It may be the last night we sleep comfortably in a bed for a long time. We should make it count."

All Arida could do again was nod as she too downed the rest of her wine in one big gulp.

"You know," Faelyn said slowly walking towards her "You can stop looking like I just asked you *to* bed." He reached down and plucked the cup from her hands. He moved with elven grace as he set the cup down with a soft thud on the night stand where it still sat against the opposite wall.

Arida watched him as he turned back to her, a warm flush heated her cheeks. "I don't know what you are talking about." She scooched to the left side of the bed and quickly untied her boots and set them down with a thud onto the wood floor. She refused to meet his gaze when he glanced back with a grin. Faelyn chuckled as he moved to the other side of the bed. Arida could feel the mattress bow as he too sat on the edge and began unlacing his own boots.

Fully clothed Arida slipped under the covers. The blankets weren't the luxurious silk sheets she was used to back home, but they also weren't the scratchy wool of the bed roll she had slept with on the ground the last few nights so she gladly snuggled down into the comfort of the bed. Faelyn stood and blew out the candles in the room, sending them into complete darkness.

The bed bowed again and she felt the blankets tug slightly as he too got under the covers. She could tell by his slower than normal movements he was being careful how close he got to her. Once he was settled she could feel his presence but no part of him was actually touching her. She could hear his breathing though, slow and even. She was paying so close attention to the rhythm of his breaths that she didn't even realize when it lulled her to sleep.

Chapter Twenty Two

Arida wasn't sure how long she had been asleep for when the sound of a loud thud followed by a sharp curse woke her with a start. Faelyn was already sitting up in bed next to her, his body was half turned and in his hand was a small dagger. She wasn't even sure where he had been keeping it in the bed with them. Footsteps quickly scurried away down the hall toward the stairs. Once she could no longer hear them Faelyn let out a small chuckle.

"I will give the inn keeper this, he's bold."

Arida couldn't hold the shudder back this time as the realization sunk in that the thud, she had heard was the door to their room hitting the metal headboard of their bed. So, Faelyn had been right to move the bed ahead of time.

Faelyn slowly laid back down, the dagger now back in whatever secret sheath pocket he had it in before.

"Try to get some more sleep, morning is still a few hours away." He said shifting slightly, trying to re-find his comfortable position Arida assumed. She followed his lead laying her head back on her pillow. But after moments of lying there in the dark and quiet Arida just couldn't find sleep. The floor creaked and cracked as more patrons headed to their rooms for the night. Each echo of footsteps had her on edge. Someone drunkenly yelled from the street below, another voice yelled back and it sounded like a fight might have broken out.

"If you don't go to sleep, you're going to fall off your horse tomorrow." Faelyn grumbled over his shoulder.

"And how did you know I wasn't asleep?" Arida responded, turning over in bed and staring at his back.

Faelyn turned and though it was pitch black she knew he had an incredulous look on his face.

"Because you are radiating stress. I think if you were any more tense you would turn into a statue."

Arida rolled her eyes. "Sorry, I am not used to so much noise around me while I sleep."

"You live in a palace, surrounded by guards walking around the hallways in steel armor. I would think you were used to sleeping through noise."

"Well, those were noises of people I knew, people I trusted..." Arida stopped realizing that it was those same guards, those same people who she was now running from.

Faelyn was still turned towards her, but his body language seemed to change and relax a little.

"Sometimes I forget." He muttered finally breaking the silence.

"Forget what?" she whispered back.

"I forget how young you are. How just a few days ago you were still at your mother's side learning about how to rule a kingdom. And now, you're running for your life after several kidnapping and assination attempts by your own uncle and being helped by a member of a blacklisted people hated by most across a continent you haven't even seen."

Arida had nothing to say back. She just stared at the darkness towards him. She also was suddenly aware of how inexperienced in the ways of the world she was. Arida prided herself on always staying strong. And though she had felt older beyond her years with all of her responsibilities at the palace, without them now she just felt, unsure of herself.

"Try to sleep. I'm here and no one is getting in." Faelyn shifted again, adjusting the blankets around them both, and started humming. The melody was gentle but loud enough that Arida was able to focus on it and not the sounds of the bustling nightlife around them.

Arida closed her eyes and listened to the song. Faelyn's humming was soothing, the song flowed smoothly like a stream. The tune not one she was familiar with, but was comforting all the same. Arida could feel herself drifting, following the tones of the song into sleep. The song still drifted through her mind in her dreams.

Chapter Twenty Three

The room was warm when Arida could feel herself begin to wake. She opened her eyes and looked at the sun streaming through the thin curtains and reflecting on the wall beside the bed. As she shifted to stretch her limbs, still stiff from the several days on horseback and her fall she was aware of a soft pressure. Glancing down at the bed she saw a strong tanned arm draped across her. She turned her head and saw Faelyn, still sound asleep laying so close she could have softly blown the few strands of red hair that had fallen across his face away from his eyes. She stared at him, studying his features closely. Now that they had been traveling outside for several days his freckles were more prominent across his nose; a nose that would have been the perfectly symmetrical feature of the elves if it hadn't been for the small bump on the bridge, most likely from being broken. His arm shifted as he stirred. It tightened for a moment around her, his fingers bunched in the blankets at her hip. If she didn't know better, she could have sworn he could sense her gaze even in sleep. When she moved her gaze slowly up his arm and back to his face, she noticed the striking gaze of his green eyes staring back at her.

"Good morning." He said pulling his arm slowly back to his side.

Arida's waist felt suddenly cool and light where his arm had been. "Um, good morning." Arida mumbled suddenly confused as to why she had been watching the elf sleep, and why she was a little sad that he had pulled himself away from her.

Faelyn sat up and pulled himself out of the bed entirely.

"We should be getting ready to go. Someone surely has found the bodies from yesterday and word will have spread to be on the lookout and watch for any newcomers into the bay. We should get supplies and get going before too many people are up and walking around the markets." He quickly laced in his boots and gestured for her to move.

Arida untangled herself from the bed and Faelyn pulled it away from the door and back to its original position. He then moved and slung his pack over his shoulder and adjusted it so it rested comfortably. There was no mention of last night's lullaby or her getting caught watching him this morning.

Arida excused herself to the common floor washroom, though its cleanliness actually made her miss the forest. After relieving herself she used the scratched piece of tin the inn was trying to pass as a mirror to rinse her face and run her fingers through her hair in place of the hair comb that went missing with her horse.

She met Faelyn at the top of the landing and headed down to the main room together. Faelyn dropped the room key at the front desk, the clerk from the night before nowhere to be seen at this early of an hour. In fact, the only other person in the room with them was an unconscious sailor draped over one of the tables. A half drank glass of ale sitting next to him.

They walked out the front door and made their way towards the small market they had seen on their way in. The sun was just coming up over the roofs of some of the shops when they made it to the first few vendors. Luckily many of the merchants were already there, ready to make sales from the travelers and sailors who leave early. They were able to quickly secure a new pack and a single bed roll in one of the first booths they entered. This was now strapped onto Arida's shoulders. The weight wasn't heavy, just bulky and a foreign feeling she wasn't yet used to.

Arida was browsing a table of small trinkets and baubles that was positioned next to a vendor who specialized in food suitable for travel. She was picking through the random assortment of items hoping to come across a replacement hair brush when she noticed Faelyn shifting himself closer and closer to her. It was when his hip grazed hers and he leaned down as if he too was admiring the small locket, she held that he whispered so quietly she doubted even the woman who was sitting on the other side of the table could hear him.

"There is a man a few stands down who I believe has been following us since we left the inn. He was hanging around across the street and has been keeping a few paces behind us since." Faelyn picked up a small ornate hand mirror and angled it. For a flash Arida caught the reflection of a man in a dark cloak standing by a table behind them. Just as the mirror tilted Arida noticed the man's gaze flick towards them.

"What do we do?" Arida whispered back slowly putting the locket down.

"We keep moving. Act like you haven't noticed him. We are going to try to pick up a few more things, hopefully soon the market will get busier and we will be able to lose him."

Arida glanced up at the elf's face "Do you really believe we can just simply lose him in the crowd?"

He met her gaze, his jaw tense. "No."

They kept moving, Arida was able to snag a hairbrush and some leather strips to tie her hair back. As Faelyn paid the man running the booth Arida tucked the procured items into his pack, using the excuse to sweep her gaze around the market.

The man in the cloak was two stalls down. He had apparently decided to give up the pretending, he was now openly staring them down.

"I want to try to get some more food before we try to lose him." Faelyn said turning around once Arida had refastened his pack.

"And how do you plan on doing that?" Though the sun had now risen it was clear to Arida that Moons Bay was not a morning town. Very few people were out still, leaving the streets empty and open.

"Just follow my lead." Faelyn moved a few more tables down pausing to pick up a few packages of dried meat. He laid a coin down on the table, not bothering to interact with the man seated behind it.

Arida followed closely, aware of Faelyn's slow increase of speed. She gripped the straps on her shoulders tightly, trying to keep the pack from bouncing around on her back. Soon it was all Arida could do to not break into a jog to keep up with the elf's long stride.

The man in the dark cloak also picked up his speed.

"This way." Faelyn said gruffly taking a sharp left away from the market and down an alley in-between a set of shops not yet open for the day. He reached back and grabbed Arida's wrist, pulling her along even faster.

The sound of their steps echoed off the walls of the buildings they went past, a third set echoed a few seconds off of theirs.

"What about horses?" Arida gasped.

"There's no time to go back. We will just have to go on foot for now." The elf shot a look back over his shoulder before he turned them again around another corner, heading further from the center of town. Arida could see the wall getting closer and closer, but as far as she could tell there was just the one gate that they had come through on the way in. And they were not running in the direction of the docks, so Arida wasn't sure what the elf's plan was.

Her wrist was sore from being tugged on and she could feel her feet pounding in her shoes from the force of striking so fast on the coble stone street. She was also unused to carrying weight on her back and the shape of the pack was odd and cumbersome thanks to the rolled-up mat tucked inside. The whole thing was becoming difficult to keep in place, especially with only one hand.

Arida glanced behind her and the man in the dark cloak had dropped back slightly thanks to Faelyn's consistent pace. He clearly didn't want to start an all-out chase in the middle of town. But the man's gaze was firmly fixed on them and he was not about to let them go easily.

"I'm going to need you to trust me." Faelyn said quickly drawing her attention back forward.

"Trust you with what?" Arida glanced around wondering what he could possibly have planned.

The wall was now coming closer into view, the buildings were getting fewer. The homes still closed up from the night.

Faelyn upped their pace again; they were now full out running. It took everything in Arida to keep her feet underneath her as she tried to keep up. Her breaths began to come out in small pants from the exertion.

The wall was now right in front of them, a solid foreboding mass.

"What are you doing?" Arida yelled, hoping to pull Faelyn's attention. But he didn't stop, didn't slow.

The wall was at least eight feet tall and made of solid brick. There was no way they could get through it. And Arida's brain was just trying to calculate what on earth the elf's plan could be when he yanked her arm so strongly, she nearly tripped and fell. But she didn't, Faelyn's other arm caught her around the waist and lifted her easily into his arms never breaking stride.

He shifted her into a cradle position tucking her close to his chest, the pack flattening between her back and his arm. The wall was only a few feet in front of them and now that Arida wasn't dragging behind him he released a full speed sprint, quickly closing the gap. The houses were a grey blur whipping past. Arida couldn't believe how fast they were now running, she couldn't decide if it was better to keep her eyes open or to close them tight.

And then she was flying.

Arida's breath caught in her throat the minute she was airborne. Faelyn had used his speed and strength to throw her up in the air. Arida watched in shock as her body soared over the wall, missing the bricks by inches. She twisted knowing full well she would never land on her feet but hoping to maybe land on her side again as she had the day before. The ground below didn't appear rocky, so hopefully she wouldn't break anything when she landed.

Something flashed in the corner of her vision and before she could blink Faelyn was now standing on the ground below her. A half a heartbeat later she was landing into his waiting arms.

The breath she had been holding finally rushed out on the impact. She looked up at the elf's face, he wasn't even breathing hard. His gaze dropped to hers for a second and then he looked up at the wall.

"I don't think he will be able to follow. But are you okay to keep running for a bit? I want to create some distance in case he has friends lurking around."

Arida nodded still breathless as Faelyn set her back on her feet. He grabbed her by the hand this time and started leading her in a jog through the woods. Arida couldn't help one last glance back to the wall. She could have almost sworn she heard the scraping sound of someone trying to climb it.

Chapter Twenty Four

Faelyn kept them at an even pace for what Arida could only assume was a few miles. They went through the woods, keeping off main trails and walking paths. The sun was high in the sky above the trees by the time he began slowing down.

After another long stretch at a quick walking speed, he slowed them to a pause in a small grouping of trees.

Arida's knees were shaking from exertion and her feet were sore in her boots. She walked over to the closest tree, discarding her pack as she went. She slumped against it, sliding down the rough trunk until she was sitting with her legs outstretched. The ground was cold and damp beneath her but she didn't care. Again, Faelyn looked as if he had just been going for a leisurely stroll through the woods and not running for miles through woodland terrain.

"What do we do now?" Arida asked, after catching her breath enough to not sound winded.

"I think our plan stays the same. We are headed in the right direction; it's just going to take us a bit longer now that we are on foot and not horseback."

"Yes, but what about supplies? I don't think the one pack of jerky and the package of tree nuts we were able to pick up is enough to get us far."

"No." Faelyn said adjusting the strap on his pack "But we should reach the Corvack river by tonight, we will be able to forage for food on the way and I can catch us some fish once we get there."

Arida just stared at him with a questioning look. "And how do you plan to do that?"

He stared back at her. "Elf, remember? I was raised in the woods; I was taught how to live off the land without help from shops or towns or people." His tone grew sharp at the end of his sentence. And Arida remembered that this wasn't the first time he was probably left in the woods with no help from anyone in the towns. His pointed ears alone were enough of a marker of untrust. And Arida had begun to forget during their time together that he was a part of a people that had gone against her family and her kingdom years ago. A people she hadn't been raised to hate, but to never fully trust.

"I had no problem catching those rabbits. Fish won't be much harder." He finished, looking around in the trees before turning back to her. Arida raise her hands up in a surrender motion.

"Anyway," He continued, "Once we meet up with the river, there should be a ferry a few miles from here that can take us across. That will bring us to the foothills of Mathwich Mountains and there are some small fishing villages spaced around the area there that we can grab a few things from before we move through the mountain passes."

Arida glanced around at the forest wondering how on earth they were going to get anywhere quickly on foot. Faelyn spoke as if it was a matter of days but Arida had studied maps of Aiden and new her realm was large, even shrunk down on paper.

"And if we are being followed? I don't know if I can keep running like that." She resisted the urge to massage her feet. The boots the Clarea shop keeper had sold her were new and slow to break in, more noticeably now that she was traveling on foot. The leather was stiff and unforgiving against her feet that were unused to bumpy unpaved terrain. But the shoes were holding up well against the scuffs and bumps she caused by not watching her footing.

The sight of the boots and the memory of the woman who sold them to her sent a wave of sadness through Arida. If it hadn't been for that interaction the curly haired shop keeper would still be alive.

"We will deal with it as it comes." Faelyn said, pulling Arida back to the present conversation. "For now, we should start moving. I want to find a place to camp near the river and as far as we can get from Moons Bay." He walked close and reached his hand out. Arida grasped it and let him pull her to her aching feet. He quickly dropped her hand and turned, beginning their long trek through the woods in a direction he seemed to instinctively know. Arida followed, scooping up her pack as she went, tucking yet another feeling of sorrow deep down to deal with later.

They had been walking slowly and for several hours navigating through the root covered terrain. Only her years of training in court etiquette kept her from complaining loudly about the ache in her feet that had moved up her calves and all the way to her thighs. Faelyn had paused here and there along the way, foraging bushes of late season berries and other plants he recognized. She had questioned him the first time. Asking if he was sure that the red berries he had packed into a small cloth were in fact edible and not poisonous. He had just looked her dead in the eye and popped a small handful into his mouth before storing the bundle into the pack and continuing on their trek. After that she chose not to question him.

The sun was just starting to dip behind the trees when Arida heard the rushing of water. They broke from the tree line onto the rocky banks of the wide and fast moving Corvack river. White caps rippled where large rocks protruded from the murky grey water. Arida felt her eyes widen as she took in yet another new experience. Other than the small pond on the castle grounds and the brief look at the sea at Moon's Bay this was the first time she had been close to a large body of water. And to witness the sheer power of it was truly something she had never thought to see. Where the sea had been gleaming and peaceful, this water was rough and tumultuous. The rushing sound of it speeding by was far louder than the gentle laps of yesterday's waves.

Arida was mindful to stay higher up at the bank. She had an instructor once who had tried to teach her to swim at her mother's insistence, but she had been too frightened of going under the water at the pond to learn much more than how to wade waste deep. Eventually she had gotten too old that her mother hadn't wanted it to become known that she refused to learn to swim and had stopped pushing her to attend the lessons. Arida wasn't sure where her fear of water came from, maybe from her mother's strong reaction after she tried to ride the water bucket down the well when she was small. But she couldn't get past the terror of it, even now as an adult.

The longer she watched the water the more she was truly mesmerized by its movement. The way it flowed and moved so freely along the rocks and the bank. Yet stayed so structured in its path. Her gaze broke when a familiar warmth radiated on her chest.

Arida broke her gaze from the water and looked down, pulling at the chain around her neck and pulling the slow heating amulet out. The red stone was swirling and moving in a similar motion as the water. When she noticed Faelyn also looking at the necklace, she quickly tucked it back into her shirt.

"Why does it move like that?" he asked, his gaze flickering from where it lay tucked away to her face.

"I'm not sure." she replied truthfully. Faelyn gave her a stern look. And his tone came out lower than normal.

"You know you can trust me, right? I think I have proven that at this stage."

Arida nervously tucked a stray strand of hair behind her ear.

"I know you have. I truly don't know why the pendant is reacting the way it is. My mother taught me that it has always been passed down in the family to the first daughter and that it was important for our kingdom that I never let it out of my sight nor let anyone see it. But more importantly she taught me that even trees can have ears and you can only speak openly in places you fully control who and what hears you. But I can promise you, if she knew how the amulet animated itself like this, she never told me."

Faelyn stared back at her, assessing the information she gave him. "Okay." He finally said, looking around them. "I say let's start heading up stream until we find a spot that will make a good camp." He turned and started walking, mindful of the smooth river rocks that were speckling the bank.

Arida followed, the necklace slowly cooling back down. "There was one thing..." She said remembering the days leading up to her fleeing. Faelyn paused and looked back at her. She knew she could trust him. But breaking a rule that had been drilled into her for years was difficult to do.

She looked around her, the forest was still a bustle with the sounds of birds and she was hoping that the roaring river was drowning out her words from anyone who may be trying to overhear.

"It started doing this the day you first saved me from the assassin in the throne room. I asked my mother about it that day and she said she had feared it was signaling the return of magic." Pausing she took a breath and continued. "She told me that she had feared magic was starting to come back in places. And that there were rumors from Gallis' spies that it was starting to be noticed. She didn't say what it had to do with the necklace but..." She looked up at the elf who was once again studying her. She still didn't trust discussing the part about the Spellborns out in such an open area, especially when it had just moments ago started signaling.

"These areas she was talking about, could those be similar to what we saw by the wall?"

Faelyn's face was stern, as if he knew she was still not telling him everything. But he answered her anyway. "I think your mother knew more than she was leading on about that necklace. It seems to be more than just a family heirloom. And is probably why Gallis is trying so hard to get to you."

Arida was slightly shocked that he had pieced that together. She hadn't told him about her and her uncle's conversation in the throne room the day he had begun to unveil his plan to take the throne. "Yes, I think so too." She replied.

"Can I ask that when it starts 'acting up' as you say, can you let me know?" He locked his eyes on hers. "It seems to know when shit is about to go down and it would be a hell of a lot easier to protect you if I was given a little warning."

A large wave broke over rocks near shore adding an ominous crash to the end of his words.

"Yes, that seems fair." Arida said with a small nod.

"We should keep going." Is all Faelyn said as he turned back and began following the river. Arida quietly followed, the necklace finally cold again.

Chapter Twenty Five

Faelyn had guided her farther and farther upstream until he found a small tree grove next to the bank he seemed to like for camp. As soon as he announced this was their stopping point Arida sagged to the ground, grateful to finally rest her feet, and shrug her pack off. She quickly went at her laces, working quickly to get her boots off. Faelyn chuckled as he set his own pack down and stretched his back. The path along the river bank had been a mixture of wet sandy mud only interrupted by an occasional camouflaged river stone that tried to make her feet slip or ankles twist. Only the deep firm tread on her boots kept her from tumbling into the wet muck. The air this close to the water was far colder than it had been when they were walking through the trees. But despite that Arida had felt sweat on her brow from the exertion of the day.

As soon as the boots were off, she quickly tucked her socks in them and stood. Gingerly she walked across the rocky sand and made her way to the rivers edge. She inched her toes closer until the frigid water nipped at them. She shivered as she dipped her feet fully into the water, it lapped gently at her shins the cold stinging like little needles but was also very soothing to her aching joints. She turned and saw Faelyn bend down; he also began unlacing his boots and joined her. Walking ankle deep into the water he closed his eyes and sighed before wading out farther.

Arida watched as he walked farther out into the river, clearly uncaring that his pants were getting soaked. He stopped when he was about mid-thigh deep. He looked around in the running water clearly on the search for something.

Quicker than she thought would have been possible Faelyn shot his hand into the river with a splash. When he pulled his arm back up a silver fish was wiggling in his closed fist. Arida watched in shock as he waded back to shore. He winked at her as he passed.

She turned still stunned and watched as he pulled a small knife out of the sheath on his belt and made quick work of killing, gutting and descaling the fish. When he had finished, he walked back to where he had dropped the bags and began preparing their camp.

Arida eventually followed, her toes now slightly numb and walked up to the grassy patch next to the tree grove, grabbing her boots and socks on the way. Just like the first nights in the woods, Faelyn started a small fire, and built another wooden stand above it. Skewering the fish like he had done before with the rabbit he set it up on the small spit to cook.

While the fish roasted Faelyn pulled out one of the small bundles of berries he had gathered on their trek through the woods and spread it out between them. He grabbed a couple and popped them into his mouth before rotating the fish a quarter turn.

"Your weirdly good at this, 'running from people and living in the woods,' thing." Arida joked grabbing a few of the berries and slowly placing them in her mouth. Their juice was sweet and reminded her of a blueberry despite their red color.

"Well, growing up I had a lot of practice. Before I joined the guard I left home for a while wanting to see what the world was like. Unfortunately being an elf, I couldn't really find a place that allowed me to stay for long." He rotated the fish again; the smell of the meat cooking was making Arida's mouth water. But she tried to focus on the small scrap of personal information Fae-lyn had just given her.

"Where is home?" She asked hoping he would reveal more. In their weeks together he had shared nothing of himself.

He gave her a sideways look like he knew exactly what she was up to. "I was born and raised in the North Forest, the homeland of the elves. That's where most of us are born except for the oldest of our kind, the ones who remember the land... differently."

Arida knew what he meant; the elves were known for their exceptionally long-life spans. A trait once thought to have been linked by their strong connection to magic. But over the past century proved not to be the case. But that comment made a thought pop into her mind.

"Wait, how old are you?" She fully turned towards him and studied his features again. He appeared no more than a few years older than herself.

"I'm young for my kind." Was his response, but when she just kept staring at him, he sighed "I'm seventy-five."

The look of shock froze on her face, making Faelyn laugh so loudly she could have sworn she heard it echo off the river.

"There's no way. You look, twenty-five... at most!"

He laughed again. "Elves age differently, our lives are long. What did you expect? That we would look like old crones for the majority of that life?"

Arida wasn't sure what she had thought. She had only met a handful of elves in her whole life, most of them were workers in the castle and none of them she had ever spoken to. Faelyn was the only one she had had regular conversations with. And even at that the majority of their time had been spent traveling in complete silence.

Faelyn reached forward and pulled the fish off the fire. He carefully pulled it off the skewer and set it on the cloth next to the berries. His face had an amused grin on it. He clearly enjoyed shocking her with his small revelation.

Seventy-five she thought. She wondered if his parents had been around during the time of Koening? If they used to tell stories to him as a child of what it had been like back then. She wondered what side they would have been on? But these questions she kept to herself, remembering that sometimes its better not to ask if the answer might be the one you didn't want.

There was no more conversation as they ate their meal. The white meat of the fish didn't have much flavor, but it calmed the grumbling in her belly. When the last of it was gone Arida leaned back in the grass and wiped her hands in the soft blades, cleaning the last of the grease from her fingers. She gently chuckled.

"What?" Faelyn asked confused by her laugh.

"I was just thinking what my mother would say if she could see me right now. I just ate a fish you caught with your bare hands with my fingers and am cleaning them off in the grass. All those years of manners and etiquette lessons for this..." She laughed and lifted her dust covered hand that had a layer of mud caked under her nails. Faelyn joined her this time, his laugh the sound of pure joy. It echoed across the calm river melding perfectly with the sounds of the birds.

When the laughter died, they both sat there and listened to the water lap gently against the beach and watched the sun slowly sink below the horizon. The sky turning from blue, to pink, and eventually stars started scattering across.

Faelyn stood, drawing Arida's gaze. He walked over to their bags and rummaged through it. He pulled out the lone bed roll they had left, since they were unable to procure a second one at the market before they had to flee.

"Here." he said handing the roll to Arida.

"Thank you." She murmured as she took the mat and placed it on the ground beside her before slowly unrolling it. Faelyn then pulled his dark green cloak out from the bag and spread it out over the ground across the fire from her. He settled down onto his makeshift bed, laying back folding his hands behind his head. He gazed up at the sky, watching the stars slowly emerge. Arida observed him for a moment before also laying on her back. They laid there together, silently watching the sky and listening to the river before slowly drifting off to sleep.

Chapter Twenty Six

The next morning Faelyn caught them another fish for breakfast. They ate it and another bundle of berries before packing up the beds. As Arida retied her shoes Faelyn worked on hiding the remnants of their fire. Smothering the coals in dirt and then arranging rocks on top so that it looked more natural.

"Ready?" He asked when she stood up, shoes securely but reluctantly back on.

"Yes." She sighed motioning for him to lead the way forward.

They trekked for most of the day following the river. There were times where outcroppings or inlets pushed them to hike up into the woods and around the obstacles before coming back down and continuing on. They had to climb over a fallen tree that slowly crumbled under Arida's hands as soon as she leaned on it to try to kick her legs over. Faelyn of course vaulted over it elegantly so he, unlike her, wasn't completely damp after from the water-logged wood. The thick material of her cloak took most of it thankfully, so Arida wasn't chilled to the bone the rest of their hike that day, but it did make the weight on her back heavier.

Faelyn foraged as they went. Handing small piles of berries to Arida to snack on as they walked so, they wouldn't lose time stopping to eat.

It was just past midday when a small structure on the river bank appeared. It looked like a malformed tree that jutted out just a few feet into the water. A small mossy hut seemed to be what attached it to the shore. Looking across there was another hut similar to the first on the opposite bank. As they approached Arida noticed an old wooden boat tethered onto what she now recognized as a dock. This was what Faelyn must have been referring to as the 'passing'. A lone man was sitting on the boat watching them as they approached.

"Don't worry." Faelyn whispered as Arida hesitated when she noticed the man. "He owns the boat; he will ferry us across the river."

They continued their approach, the man standing when they reached the steps to the dock.

"Afternoon." The man said in a gruff tone and inclined his head in their direction. He was older, with a white beard and matching strands of thin white hair that poked out from under a knit cap on his head. His face showed the lines of age but his eyes were sharp and clearly missed nothing.

"How much for the ferry?" Faelyn asked gesturing to the boat.

"Three copper coins each." The man said, his eyes raked up and down Arida making her uncomfortable in more than one way with the attention. Her cheeks burned at the memory of Faelyn's afore mentioned observation about her reaction to the attention of men. She glanced up and swore she saw a flash of a smile before his face was stoic once more. This only made her cheeks burn hotter. She turned her face away slightly, hoping the ferryman didn't also notice her reaction.

Faelyn pulled the asked for money out of his pocket and dropped it into the ferry mans outstretched hand. He did a quick count of his procurement before dropping it into a leather pouch on his belt. He stepped to the side and waved his hand, directing them onto the boat.

It wasn't a large vessel. Just the right size to withstand the small rapids yet not drag across the bottom. The boat rocked slightly when Faelyn stepped on. He moved to the side and offered a hand to Arida. She took it carefully as she slowly boarded. The wood creaked under her weight in a non-reassuring way.

The captain followed them onboard and silently worked on the ropes that were holding the boat to the dock. As soon as they were free, the man grabbed a large pole with a wide paddle on the bottom and pushed them off from shore. He used the pole to steer them in the direction of the second hut. Occasionally he would dip the pole in and use the current to navigate them around large rocks or debris, but for the most part the direction of the swirling water in the rapids kept them moving across.

The shore on the other side of the river had not looked too far away when they had been standing on land. Now bobbing at the mercy of the waves it seemed miles away. According to the ferryman it would take almost twenty minutes for the crossing.

When they were almost halfway through the crossing Arida felt the amulet prickle against her chest. She twisted her head to look back at the bank they had left. Just as she searched for the reason of the disturbance the first arrow zipped past her head, missing her by mere inches.

"Get down!" Faelyn yelled lunging forward and shoving Arida to the deck of the boat. Another arrow flew by this time striking the wooden slat right where Faelyn had just been standing. Arida popped her head up enough to see two men emerge from the trees behind them and walk to the edge of the dock. Both had bows in their hands aiming arrows at the vessel. The man on the left Arida recognized as the same one who had chased them from Moon's Bay. Faelyn had been right; he did have friends waiting for him. And now they both were standing on the dock trying to sink the boat in the middle of the river.

Arida felt like a rock just sank to her gut as another volley of arrows came at them. One of which struck home in the back of the ferry man who had crouched near the bow with the pole still in his hand from trying to direct them through the growing rapids. The man slumped forward as soon as the arrow hit. Arida released a small scream as the body slumped against the deck. The pole tumbled from his hand into the water below.

"Shit." Faelyn grumbled crouching half over Arida, blocking her from any stray arrows. The boat rocked, a rapid pushing them off course easily now that there was no one to redirect it. Another two thuds sounded, hitting nowhere near them now that the boat wasn't keeping a steady course. Faelyn popped his head up high enough to take a look at the direction they were headed.

"Shit!" He yelled again.

"You really need to stop saying that." Arida yelled back, the sound of the river suddenly getting louder. She popped her head up too so she could see what he was clenching his jaw and helplessly looking around the empty boat over.

"Shit!" she parroted; the current had pulled the small boat right into a very large grouping of raging rapids. White foam was even floating on top of the water where it churned and swirled around. The boat hit the first section of angry waves and sent the occupants pitching forward.

Faelyn grabbed Arida before her head could hit the wooden bottom of the boat. But before she could thank him, the water shoved them again. Arida rolled onto her side, the force of the impact jarring her spine making her teeth rattle. A stinging coolness splattered on her cheek. Looking up she could see water beginning to splash over the edge, the wood growing dark.

"Faelyn!" Arida yelled pointing to what she saw. He looked up from where he had been crouched and she could see fear flash on his eyes as more water splashed over a small pool growing in the bottom of the boat. She had never told her guard about her incompetence in the water and dread weighed like a stone in her belly at the very real realization they both could end up in the water. They pitched again, Faelyn who had been trying to get up to get back over to her stumbled. Arida watched in horror as the normally graceful elf was caught off guard by his bodies sudden change in direction. He took a step back to try to regain his balance. But what happened instead caused Arida to yell out. Already near the edge of the boat there was nowhere for him to step to slow himself as he reeled back. Arida watched in horror as his body toppled over the side of the boat into the water.

One minute he was there and the next he was gone accompanied by a large splash. Arida scrambled on her hands and knees and pulled herself to the edge and looked over into the water below. She whipped her head back and forth looking for any sign of the elf.

She saw nothing, no sign of him. No flash of red hair, no movement other than that of the water itself it had completely swallowed him without a trace.

Without her partner's weight the boats rocking increased dramatically. Full waves crashed in, drenching Arida in the freezing water. She was trying her best to counterbalance her weight with that of the dead ferryman's. Leaning away from the direction the boat was taking while also still searching for any signs of Faelyn. Her muscles ached in protest to the strain she was putting on them in her attempts to stay in. Arida was leaning forward when the boat hit yet another rapid and instead of shoving her back, the boat flipped forward. A small scream left Arida's mouth just before she was dumped from the boat and into the water.

It seemed to reach up and surround her in its shockingly cold grasp. Immediately all of her breath was sucked from her lungs causing a small stream of air bubbles to fly away from her towards the surface as it pulled her down into the depths of the river.

Arida fought against the dark water, struggling to find the surface, to follow that string of bubbles. Finally, her head broke through the surface for a second, she gasped for air and threw her hands out slapping the water, hoping to stay afloat. She was able to stay up for a moment before another rapid shoved her back down. She flipped and tumbled bumping rocks and other debris as she went. Her lungs burned, aching for oxygen. She tried kicking and moving her arms the way her teacher had tried to show her. But she couldn't seem to find the water's surface again. Her back cracked against something sharp and the last hope for air began to fade.

Just as she was about to give up the pull of the water lessened, and the visibility became clearer. The thick sand and silt that had been swirling around her started to settle. She must have been towed far enough over she had escaped the worst of the rapids.

A small glimmer in the water caught her eye and she kicked hard. Her back was sore and caused a slight tingle in her legs as she worked her oxygen deprived muscles hard to get to the surface. Her face felt the air first as she once again broke through. Her lungs gratefully took in the air, gasping and choking it down. She blinked hard trying to clear the water still streaming off her hair out of her eyes. As it cleared, she noticed a outstrip of land poking out in front of her. Still coughing she worked to try to propel her body through the water towards it. Kicking and pulling the water with her arms and legs.

Slowly she made it closer and closer until she felt the grittiness of sand under her hands, and her kicking feet struck something solid. Grabbing ahold of it she pulled herself up and onto the beach until most of her body was out of the frigid rivers grasp. She flipped over on her back her body shaking from exhaustion and lack of oxygen, her vision growing dark around the edges.

A shadow passed over her and she turned her head just in time to see the edge of a dark cloak before something solid struck against the side of her head and her world went dark.

Chapter Twenty Seven

Arida was aware of a noise before anything else. It sounded like footsteps, pacing back and forth. A slight echo followed them, almost rough sounding. Like they weren't walking on polished floors but rugged stone. Eventually a second set of footsteps joined and the first scuffed to a stop, she could hear the sound of pebbles skittering across the floor. When the second footsteps also stopped, the voices began.

"Has she woken up yet?" The first male voice said, his voice also echoed slightly at the end.

"Not yet." A gruff, also male, second voice replied. Arida didn't recognize either of them.

"When will Gallis be here to collect her?" The second man asked. Arida's brain froze at the mention of her uncle's name.

"I got word to a carrier; it should take a day to get to him and I assume he will make quick work of the journey to come get her." The first voice replied.

"And until then?"

"We have our orders. Try to get as much information from her as possible. Gallis was pretty clear he has no care for his niece anymore. He simply wants information and for her and all her affects to be handed over to him. So, that's what we will do. Who knows, Gallis may be so grateful for the information we get from her. He may promote us."

"Now if the spoiled brat would just wake up..."

Arida was aware of feeling slowly returning to her body, her physical senses now catching up to her mental ones. She felt a tight pressure on her wrist. Her shoulders were strained and the muscles felt like they were bunched into a ball. Her hands were numb, as if blood had stopped flowing to them a long time ago.

She tried to fight consciousness as long as she could. Fearful for what was waiting for her when she did wake up. But unfortunately, her body wouldn't listen to her and she felt her eyes flutter open.

Dark pressed around her. She blinked slowly, trying to allow her eyes to adjust. Shapes became recognizable a wall of rocks in a natural formation all around her. Small boulders littered around. A cave, she was in a cave. The muscles in her shoulders spasmed and as she tried to roll out the feeling her movement was restricted. Arida raised her gaze to see her hands were indeed bound and hooked. Metal cuffs were locked around her wrists, attached to a thick chain that was secured with a steel bolt through the cave ceiling. It hung just long enough that her toes just slightly grazed the rock floor below her. She also soon was reminded she was not alone. Two men stood before her in the shadows, staring at her with slick smiles plastered on their faces that made Arida's skin crawl.

"Well, look who finally decided to wake up." The man to the left said. She recognized his voice as man one from earlier. Arida said nothing, just stared down her captures.

"What, got nothing to say?" Man, number two said sneering at her. She just stared back, mastering her face into the cool uncaring face of a royal princess she had spent years perfecting. She moved her chin up just slightly, enough for them to get the point. She had a small moment of pleasure to see just how much the small movement bristled them. The smug smiles sliding off their ugly faces.

"Well, no worries love." Man one said moving closer to her. "We'll get you talking soon..."

Man number two grinned and moved closer as well.

Arida's flesh felt like it was on fire. The crack of the whip echoed again through the cave and Arida arched her body in response. Her teeth clashed together and she hissed out air between them. The chains on her wrist cut deeper into the skin.

"Come on, love." The first man said popping his head around so that she could see him. Her hair had fallen out of its braid and laid stringy from sweat on either side of her face. "Just tell me where you and your little elf friend were going and I'll give you a break." He reached up and stroked a piece of hair from her face so that he could see her better.

Arida glared at him from the corner of her eye. "How about you drop dead." Arida gritted out and pulled her face from his rough fingers. The man's face hardened and he disappeared behind her. She felt the sting of the whip against her back before she heard its crack echo through the cave again, and again.

"It's been hours and she hasn't said a damn word! Not about where they were, where they were going or anything good!" The second man yelled from the corner where he had been watching the first man work. In the hours in the cave the men had yet to address each other by names other than 'hey' so Arida was acknowledging them in her head as Ugly (man one) and Uglier (man two).

"She'll break eventually." Ugly said cracking the whip again. Arida felt her vision blur, the pain started fading into the back of her mind. She would soon lose consciousness again. She had once already, the men had been furious that they had to wait for her to wake up before doing anymore. They had shown their displeasure by ripping her clothes to shreds with the blades they kept at their waists. A tactic in trying to break her down mentally.

Unfortunately for them, she didn't give them the satisfaction they had been looking for then either. The way she looked at it, if she hadn't shown a reaction for Faelyn seeing her naked on the floor of her bathing room, then why should she care about these two thugs seeing her in tatters. Besides, all Arida could think or care about was the pain. She didn't have the mental capacity to worry about anything else. That's when they had started with the whip again.

One thing Ugly and Uglier never had thought of before trying to breakdown a member of the royal family was what training she might have received to fight against it. Her mother couldn't get herself to teach her daughter that particular skill. But she did know the importance for her to learn how to fight against torture should she be kidnapped. So, like with swimming, she had hired a teacher to do it.

Though that teacher was not allowed to cause harm to Arida in a way that made a mark -it wouldn't due to have a bruised and bloodied princess- the teachers lessons had been thorough and unlike swimming, was doing Arida well today.

When Arida woke again the men were huddled together on the other end of the cave. Ugly had something in his hand that they were talking very excitedly over. It took a second for Arida's vision to focus on what it was, but when it did her entire body stiffened. She recognized the large red stone encased in gold hanging from the thick chain. Her neck felt light and she looked down just to verify that the amulet was in fact no longer hanging against her chest. The bare ribbons of her clothes covered very little of her so she wasn't surprised that they had finally seen it.

Uglier glanced over and saw her eyes on them. He nudged his counterpart and when he too noticed Arida was awake he tucked the necklace away into a pocket in his vest.

"Good, we can start again." They moved towards her. "I think we should try another question. Since your little elf friend clearly died in the Corvack." Arida tried to hide her emotions from her face but something must have slipped through because the goon smiled widely.

"I mean, why else would he not be here trying to get you. You've been with us for hours."

"Or he's just glad to finally be rid of you." Uglier chuckled.

Arida ground her teeth together to try to keep her from snapping at them. Rule number one; her teachers voice echoed in her head, don't ever say a word. No matter what. Every word gives them an edge you may regret later.

She'd technically already broke that by telling Ugly to drop dead. But Arida felt that was an acceptable breach.

"You know, I'm growing tired of the whip. My arm kind of hurts from all the swinging." He grinned at Arida. "There is a new method I think you will really enjoy." The men walked away and began building something on the floor. It was when one of them struck a flint that she realized it was a small fire they had constructed.

Arida watched as the flames began. The fire grew and grew until one of the men grabbed a long metal object from a large pile of things the men had dumped earlier. The same pile the whip had come from. They stuck the rod into the flames and left it there for several minutes. Arida understood exactly what it was for the moment the one end began to glow. Arida closed her eyes and steeled herself, waiting for the new fresh hell to begin.

Chapter Twenty Eight

A rida couldn't help but let out a long piercing scream when the white-hot poker was pressed and held against her side. The pain was blinding, she couldn't tell if her skin was burning or melting off of her.

"Just answer the question." One of the men, Arida couldn't tell them apart anymore asked. Arida couldn't even remember the question they had asked her, though they had asked several times. Each time she refused; they would stick her with the poker. Her back had become so ravaged they had moved on to the skin on her sides.

"What is so important about the stupid necklace?" The man growled.

That's right, they wanted to know about the necklace. Word had come from a messenger at some point while they were preparing the poker. He had reported that Gallis was on his way and had a list of questions he expected to be answered by the time he reached the cave. They were still on question one. And the duo was growing more agitated by the minute that they had made no progress. Arida's flesh radiated heat from the hours of abuse and sweat mixed with the blood, stinging the open wounds.

The poker was back in the fire to reheat. In the meantime, the two men were back huddled together in the corner talking. Her guess was trying to come up with a plan if she didn't start spilling information soon. Arida glanced around the cave. Now that there was some light from the fire Arida could make out small details around her. A large table sat against one wall where her pack that she must have been able to keep with her during her swim was now dumped out and rummaged through. A few more random bits of furniture were strewn about. Partnered with the bolted chains

Arida surmised this cave was one of the cache's hidden around Aiden to be used as needed by soldiers or her uncles' men when needed. The entrance of the cave had turned out to be what Arida had thought to be another cave wall ahead of her. No light still came in through the cave opening, so the sun must not have risen yet.

Where was Faelyn? Her mind reeled through all the possibilities. Did he make it out of the river? Had he gotten taken by the men who had been firing arrows at them? Because dumb and dumber were definitely not them. Or were they right? Did Faelyn die in the river? Arida had not seen him surface before she herself had been dumped in. Her thoughts were spiraling over all the things that could have happened to him when motion caught her attention.

There was just a flash over by the curve in the cave wall where Arida assumed it opened up into the forest. The flash was quick, there one second and then gone in another. She was doubting if she really had seen anything when it flashed again; a small streak of red from the edge of the cave to the other. Just when she thought she may be hallucinating the red streak began to slow down, its movements taking shape. The silhouette of a man began to move stealthily out of the shadows as if he had been made from them. But this shadow had red hair that moved as if it had a life of its own.

Like a bright lit flame in the night, Faelyn strode in to the center of the cave, unhurt and whole. Arida watched in amazement as he stalked near, the picture of wrath illuminated by fire light. She had never seen such rage on his face before. His red hair streamed behind him as if it was flame. His lips turned into a snarl and Arida could have sworn he growled as he pulled a sword out from the sheath that lay down his back. The men heard the sound of the releasing steal and turned in unison.

It always stunned Arida just how fast elves could move. Faelyn had Ugly on the floor bleeding out in a breath's time. And in the next, Uglier was pinned with the blade of the vengeful elf's sword pressed against his throat. In fact, Arida had to blink several times just to assure herself that what was happening was real, and not a hallucination brought on by blood loss and pain.

"Give me the key." Faelyn growled. His tone holding such an animalistic roughness it was hard to believe it came from a man. She had grown so used to Faelyn during their travels she had nearly forgotten that he was in fact, not a human man. Yes, he had shown displays of speed and strength in front of her before. But he had always followed it up with a snide comment, or that half smirk he loved to use on her so much. But now there was no way she could look at him and not see the otherworldly creature he really was. Every inch of him radiated the ancient power it was lored the elves were born from. Not magic, just pure power.

His ears twitched, as if listening for any other men that may be hidden in the cave depths. His muscles rippled under the taught fabric of his shirt as he pushed the blade of his sword harder against her captor's throat.

Uglier shook at the sight of his companion on the ground, dead before he had known what or who had done it. The sword pressed harder still against the man's throat, drawing a small trail of blood. He reached into his pocket and pulled out a small metal key. In one quick move the man was dead and the key was in Faelyn's hand.

The man didn't even have a chance to scream before he slumped to the ground bleeding out.

Arida blinked again slowly and Faelyn was right in front of her. She studied his face, his expression still furious but his eyes softened as he took in her gaze. He moved his hands to the lock that was holding her hands to the chain above her head. She heard the click of the lock coming undone and then felt all of her body weight pitch forward. Following the momentum of her deadened arms.

Faelyn caught her with ease. Carefully supporting her weight with one arm around her waist as the other reached up and cradled the back of her dropping head. Arida gasped as all the blood that had drained from her arms over the past hours rushed back to them. This provided both sweet relief and excruciating pain simultaneously. It wasn't until she heard Faelyn softly murmur and shush her that she realized she had started crying. He repositioned her so that she was cradled in his arms. His face had softened even more, though everything was once again going hazy. The pain from the feeling going back to her arms partnered with her ravaged body that felt like the poker was pressing into her at the same moment the whip was fileting her back open was quickly becoming overwhelming.

Faelyn must have seen from her face she was fading fast. He stood easily with her in his arms and was beginning to head for the mouth of the cave.

"Wait." Arida was able to squeak out between silent sobs. "The necklace!" Her voice was getting garbled and she could taste blood. She was afraid he hadn't understood her, but quickly he turned and went back.

"Where?" He whispered softly to her, as if he was afraid, she would shatter completely if he spoke at full volume.

"V-vest po-po-pocket." Arida got out her gaze glancing over to the first man Faelyn had slain. He moved swiftly, using his foot to flip the dead man over. He was able to support Arida's full weight with one arm and used the other to rifle through the vest pocket, retrieving the necklace. It flashed in the warmth of the fire light and the site of it free from her uncles' men sent a sense of relief through Arida. Faelyn tucked it safely away into one of his own pockets before he readjusted Arida to hold her with both arms again.

Arida was able to hold onto awakeness long enough for them to exit the cave. But as soon as she felt the chilled night air brush against her inflamed cheek, she couldn't keep her eyes open anymore and she allowed the pain to pull her into unconsciousness.

Chapter Twenty Nine

Arida felt a comforting cooling sensation that contradicted the fire burning heat of earlier as she began to stir. Tingling stabs of pain that reminded her of the dull ache of hitting her elbow on a table, but a million times worse, radiated though her upper half. Her senses were having a hard time sorting through all the information her tortured body was signaling to her brain, causing a fog to linger just before she could fully open her eyes.

Arida's eyes fluttered open, though this time opening them to a new surrounding was a very different feeling from the last. This time she knew she was safe, especially since the moment her eyes opened there was a pair of shockingly green ones directly in her line of sight.

His whole body seemed to slump in relief. He bowed his head for a moment before looking back at her, a lock of hair that had strayed from its bindings shifted across his forehead.

"Welcome back." He rasped, his voice tight and tired from lack of sleep. She could see rare shadows under his eye.

Arida gazed around trying to take in her surroundings. They were in a small rock outcropping, different from the deep cave that had been her torture chamber. She could clearly see the sky off to the side, but a small rock ledge protruded out above them offering some coverage. A small fire burned nearby, big enough to fight the chill in the air but not big enough to throw a ton of smoke in the air and alert every one of their presence.

"Arida?" Faelyn's voice drew her attention back to him. "How are you feeling?"

She stared at him, trying to decipher for herself what she was feeling.

"I'm not sure." Her voice cracked, dry from going so long without water. Faelyn heard it too.

"Here." he said and picked up a water skin from beside them in one hand while he gently cradled her head up in the other.

She took several small sips, letting the cool water run down her sore throat. The feeling was so soothing she wanted to moan. She nodded at Faelyn to indicate she was all done with the water for now. But she shifted her weight, she wanted to sit up.

"I don't think that's a good idea. I did what I could but your back is still pretty torn up."

Arida chose not to listen to him and pulled her arms up her sides to try to use them to help support her weight. Faelyn sighed at her stubbornness but assisted her into a sitting up position.

Every muscle she had screamed in protest. Her arms almost gave out on her completely. She could feel several things tugging that she could only imagine was scabbed, healing flesh, upset at the movement. She could swear she could feel every lash flare up again as she shifted.

He used his pack to prop her up and help support her. The canvas was rough against her wounds, but her muscles appreciated the assistance in keeping her up. She glanced down at herself and was glad to see she was being covered up by Faelyn's dark green cloak. The amulet was also back around her neck which gave her an extreme sense of relief.

Her memory of the torture was becoming clearer as the fog in her mind lifted, as was her rescue. She could still see the look of utter rage on Faelyn's face as he drove his blade through those men. But everything that happened after was a complete mystery to her.

"How long was I out?" She asked her voice coming out a little easier. She rubbed absently at the bruises on her wrists.

"A full day." Faelyn answered stacking another piece of wood on their fire.

Arida nodded looking out of the sky, still trying to decipher the sensations and where all the pain areas were and how on earth they were going to get anywhere with her in this condition.

"Please don't do that." Faelyn said staring her down.

"Don't do what?" Arida asked pulling herself out of her mind and turning her gaze to him. His expression had a sadness to it she hadn't seen before. It tugged at something inside her chest that she couldn't quite place her finger on. A feeling she wasn't used to having.

"Crawl inside yourself and put your wall up. I worked hard to get you to open up over the time we have spent together. Don't block me out again, and please stop that incessant nodding."

Arida studied his face, seeing the sincerity there had her walls crack a little bit.

"I'm sorry." She whispered "Closing out the world is all I know. And I spent the last I don't even know how long fighting to keep everything in, it's hard to turn that off now."

Faelyn's face hardened, his shoulders tensed and he curled his hands into tight fists showing a glimpse of the wrath she had seen that night.

"No, I'm sorry. I tried to get to you. I surfaced just as the boat tipped you out. But you went under and I didn't see you come back up. I fought against the current, and when you finally did pop back up, the water had drawn you to the opposite side of the river from me. The two idiots who had been firing at us in the boat ambushed me as soon as I got to shore. I was fighting them off when you must have made it to the bank." He paused for a breath and Arida gave him a moment as he fought to keep inside whatever emotion he was trying to hide.

"I didn't see them take you. By the time I got over there you were gone. So, it took me awhile to track you three through the woods. Those morons must have wandered all over those woods making false trails. Once I caught the right one and tracked it to the cave, they had you chained up and were torturing you for information."

Arida chuckled darkly. "Yeah, that part I remember. "

Faelyn stared back at her his eyes looked haunted by the memory of what he had seen.

"It wasn't so bad." Arida tried to assure him. But Faelyn shot her one of his incredulous looks. "Okay it was really, really bad. Where did you get the sword by the way?" Arida nodded her head towards the blade that lay next to Faelyn's pack.

"I found it." Was the only explanation he gave, standing before she could give him a look and force him to explain further.

He grabbed a small bundle of fresh berries he had waiting off to the side and handed it to her, careful to not remove his hand until he was sure she had a good hold of it.

"Here. Eat these, it will help."

"Where are we?" Arida asked between bites of berries. The fruit was helping fade away the iron taste that was left over in her mouth.

"The foothills of the Mathwich Mountains. They brought you here, but had kept you on the east side of the North Twin. Probably to keep you hidden but to also allow Gallis to get there quicker if he had been at the palace. I brought you as far over as I could, I figured they had alerted your uncle and I wanted to get you far from him. But you were in pretty bad shape so I couldn't go as far as I had wanted to. There was no point in continuing to run when you were leaving a blood trail anyone with half a brain could track."

"Well, I feel a lot better, so you made the right choice." Arida shifted and suppressed the flinch. Her teeth grinding the berry in her mouth to pulp.

"Yeah, I'm sure." Faelyn said glaring at her. "I did what I could to tend to the worst of your injuries. They did a number on your back. It took a while to get your wounds to finally clot. But I was able to clean them out pretty well and I luckily had healing salve in my bag I had grabbed from Clarea for a 'just in case' moment. Your back is still pretty bad, but your burns seemed less angry after a few applications. If I could find the right plants or knew more about healing I could do more. But..." He shrugged his shoulders and another expression Arida hadn't seen on him before appeared on his face. He looked, helpless. Sad at the little he was able to do.

"Thank you." Was all Arida could get out. Unsure of what else to say to help with their current situation. She was unused to trying to comfort others, all of this a new feeling for her as well. They sat in silence for a few minutes, the fire popping and crackling beside them. Arida had never wished for a mirror more than she did now so that she could see for herself what her body looked like. She tried to ignore that once again Faelyn had seen her naked in a very unflattering way. Which reminded her.

"So, what am I supposed to do about clothes?" Arida asked in a way to try to lighten the mood. She looked back down at the cloak, still thankful for it but very aware that she was completely naked beneath it. The shreds that were her clothes had disappeared.

"There is a small village nearby, I planned on sneaking over there when you were awake and able to hide yourself should someone come snooping. I'll pick up new clothes and a new cloak for you and then if there's time, I'll grab the supplies we need to keep going." Arida remembered her packs contents laid out on the table in the cave, all of it once again left behind in their hurry to escape.

"Well, I'm awake now. I think if the need really arose, I could crawl to a solid hiding spot. And I would really like to no longer be naked." She stared at him pointedly.

"Okay, so I guess you would like me to go now." His normal amused expression coming back.

"Yes please."

"Wow." He exaggerated "I even got a please. Now I'll have to go." He stood slowly as Arida attempted to cross her arms and glare at him. Though all she managed to do was screw her face up in pain and grind her teeth when the movement of pulling her shoulders caused one of the wounds on her back to open back up. She could feel the blood slowly slide down her back. Faelyn's nostrils flared at the scent of the blood and he rolled his eyes.

"Now you've done it." He said and squatted back down beside her. He gently pushed against her arm, rolling her onto one shoulder so he could see her back.

She felt a coolness she recognized from when she first woke up.

"What is that?" she asked trying to peak over her shoulder.

"Stop that." He scolded focusing on what he was doing. "You're going to open up another one. And it's the salve I mentioned, it will help with healing and it seals up wounds." He slowly lowered her back down, adjusting the cloak so it didn't slip too far down her chest.

"Thank you, again." Arida said careful not to move her arms again.

"So much for crawling to safety. Are you sure you want me to go?" Faelyn asked.

"I am sure I would like to be clothed." Arida replied. The coolness had faded as had the feeling of the blood running down her skin.

"Fine, fine. I'll go." Faelyn made sure there was plenty of water within reach and a fresh bundle of fruit next to it. After Arida assured him he would be better off keeping his new found sword with him and agreeing to keep one of his knives hidden under the cloak. He finally

headed off into the woods towards the village he had
seen on their way in.

Chapter Thirty

Rage erupted from Gallis when he entered the cave and saw the two bodies of his men. Blood pooled around them and stuck to his boots and he walked around to examine what had happened here.

The men were slaughtered, that was for sure. He could tell the rage of the attack by how their necks were slashed so deep their heads were almost severed.

"The fools must not have dispatched the elf as thoroughly as they had thought." He grumbled to himself before turning to investigate the rest of the cave.

A third spot on the floor had the presence of blood, not a singular large pool, but small areas where you can tell it dripped from someone. The sight brought a sort of happiness to Gallis at the thought this was probably from his niece. How he wished he could have been here in time to see the proud and arrogant daughter of the king and queen brought down to what he was sure was the crying sniveling mess she was after the hours at his men's hands.

"Search the surrounding forests." Gallis ordered to the men he had waiting for him at the entrance. "They can't have gone far." The sound of footsteps was his answer as the men spread out to search.

He looked around some more but found nothing of interest other than the tools the men presumably used dirty and discarded on the floor like the bodies. And a discarded pack her presumed had been his nieces. Though nothing of its contents told him where his niece had been or was going. And the one item he was looking for was also absent.

Gallis turned to leave and a dark shadow filled the mouth of the cave where his men had been moments before. He froze as the darkness crept closer, filling into the nooks and crevices of the cave, searching.

"It's not here." Gallis said and he felt the shadow still. "I doubt she would have left it behind, and the elf has to know about it by now, though I doubt either of them have figured out yet what it truly does." He felt his magic prickle, rise up in response to the shadow as it closed in around him. Suddenly he felt it being pulled from him, the shadow ensconced him completely as it drained his power. Gallis fell to his knees, the pain making him want to scream, but he was becoming used to it as well. He held on and bit back his yells until the pull finally lessoned and the shadow pulled back. A dark menacing hiss echoed around him before the darkness fully left the cave.

"Find it."

Chapter Thirty One

A rida dozed off and on while she waited for Faelyn to come back. Even if she had wanted to stay awake there was nothing she could do in the state she was in, and the boredom alone would have dragged her to sleep. But even so, her body needed the rest. The fire was warm, Faelyn had made sure there was enough wood to burn through his time gone. And she watched the flames dance and flicker until it lulled hers into sleep, the memory of a lullaby floating through her dreams.

She spent much of the time waiting for Faelyn to return in a rotation of awake and watching the fire, or napping beside it. When she was awake, she would sip on her water and snack on the food that was left for her. Though she was careful not to overdo it in case her hollow stomach rejected it. When she slept her dreams were filled with whip cracks and flashes of white-hot pain that would rouse her awake again within a few minutes.

The sun had transitioned from its position high in the sky as it could manage for this time of year to just sinking down behind the horizon when Faelyn came out from behind a tree. A new pack was strung across his back. It's bulkiness a sign that his trip was successful.

"Welcome back." Arida said grinning at Faelyn as he got closer.

"Thank you." He replied and she could tell he eyed the amount of food that was left next to her. And if she had any money on her she would have bet it that his next move would be to find a way to pick up the water skin and check how much of it was left as well.

She choked back laughter as he dropped his pack next to her and picked up the water skin. He raised a brow at her as he unscrewed the cap and took a drink. She just shook her head and looked toward the pack.

Bending down he unfastened the flap and pulled out a small bundle of clothes. He set them gingerly on her lap and allowed her to unfold them and examine his choices.

He had been smart, finding colors and materials close to what she had picked out herself at the first shop. These were a little thicker fabric, more useful here in the higher, colder elevation. It was as she shifted to try get her arm into the shirt that she realized this was not going to work out well for her. Any way she tried to bend her arms would flash pain down her back and sides.

Faelyn looked at her amused, already aware of what she was just figuring out.

"Would you like some help?" he asked.

"No, I want to just sit here and fight with this shirt for a while... I thought it would be a fun way to pass the time while I heal." Arida snapped, frustrated at the situation.

"Okay, okay, miss grumpy." He knelt beside her and grabbed the shirt from her hands. He scrunched the material of the first sleeve up as tight as he could make it and gestured for her to move her hand towards it. As she did, he slowly slid the sleeve up her arm. He then repeated the movement for the second arm. As soon as both arms were fully covered, he slowly lifted them above her head. The movement was painful, the muscles unhappy since they had been hung in that same position for so long.

Faelyn quickly pulled the shirt over her head and down her torso. He had the decency to allow the fabric of the shirt to slide down the cloak, leaving her minimally exposed.

The pants he had picked out were slightly different than the ones she had earlier. These were made out of a softer material. And Arida realized the reason for the change as he helped thread her feet through the leg holes of them.

The fabric gave easier as he pulled. It allowed him to work it over the worst of the burns and whip marks on her calves and thighs. He stopped mid-thigh and turned around so she could pull them up the rest of the way herself. He had left the waist band just high enough that she was able to grab it with her finger tips, keeping her from having to bend to grab it.

As soon as she was fully covered Faelyn took his cloak back and set it to the side. He grabbed the new pair of socks and quickly rolled them onto her feet. He thankfully kept her shoes off for now, seeing as she couldn't walk yet there wasn't much point in them.

Her shoes had been the one thing he hadn't had to buy. The tough leather had made it through the beating with nothing more than a few whip marks. The goons had thankfully not thought to use the brand or whip on her feet and therefore had not cut them off like the rest of her clothing. Faelyn had cleaned the blood from them and had them resting to dry near the fire. Arida was glad she wouldn't have to break in new boots again. It had been hard enough to do before when she was uninjured. To do so now would definitely slow them down and out them at risk of being caught.

Arida felt more comfortable now that she was clothed, the fabric was soft and gentle against her injured skin. But thick enough to fight the chill once they started moving.

Faelyn handed over a smaller dark green cloak, the color matching his own. It was made out of a thick woolen material, clearly made for those who live near the constant chill of the Twins. Tucking the new one tightly around her lap she watched Faelyn fold his cloak into a cushion shape and settle onto it beside her.

They watched the sun fade in amicable silence. The sky behind the tree tops slowly turning from blue, to faint pinks and oranges to the dark of night. Just as the first stars started to twinkle above the tallest tree Arida could feel exhaustion pulling her back towards sleep again. She was already slumped against Faelyn's pack and she could feel her head slowly lull to the side as her eyes grew heavy.

Gentle hands slowly supported her and pulled the pack away, guiding her back down onto her makeshift bed. She once again felt that cooling sensation rush over her wounds. The relief it caused pulled her fully into the depths of sleep without a wonder to its origin.

Chapter Thirty Two

Arida's dreams were plagued with the cracking of whips and the smell of burning skin. The amulet was hot against her chest, she glanced down and could see it pulsing against her ravaged skin. The inside of the stone swirled and glinted. The dark faceless figure before her pulled the whip back before releasing it with a crack again. She knew she couldn't take his administrations for much longer. Her strength was fading, the chains holding her arms above her head bit into her skin causing small lines of blood to trail down her arms, matching the rest of her body.

Just as the tip of the whip touched her skin Arida felt her body jolt awake. Her muscles tense, her teeth clamped together to prevent the scream building in her throat from releasing. White light pulsed around her, emanating from the amulet tucked under her new clothes. Clothes that were now drenched in sweat. The muscles and wounds on her back screamed in protest. Pure adrenaline kept her from collapsing back to the ground.

Arida clasped at the heat seeping into her skin allowing its familiarity to ground her. She focused around her, trying to find the whip wielder, still not convinced what she had just experienced was a dream.

Her eyes scanned, looking for any sign of movement, any sign of that flicking whip. A figure crouching across from her sent a chill down her spine even the amulets' heat couldn't fight. Her once scorched, sweaty skin turned to ice as she locked eyes with the figure. The white light pulsed in response, as if it too sensed the man.

"Easy there." The figure said in a calm tone. He slowly raised two empty hands towards her. "It's just me." The voice was familiar, comforting. Her memories flashed to the voice murmuring to her as it undid the chains that held her. And like the relief she felt then, Arida felt the last dregs of the nightmare slowly fade away into the dark night.

What had once appeared as the dark cave, opened up into the night sky. The small rock outcropping blotted out the stars directly overhead. The small fire Faelyn had worked to keep going during their time here was now just a small pile of smoldering embers.

Slowly her muscles relaxed and she loosened her grip from the chain around her neck. The white light faded, and as it did, the figure's shape became clearer as her eyes adjusted to the darkness. He shifted, more comfortable now that the light was gone.

"Faelyn?" Arida whispered, her throat dry and raw.

"Yeah, it's me." He stood and moved towards her. Closing the distance in a few strides before settling down onto one knee in front of her.

"It was just a nightmare." Arida said out loud. More as a confirmation to herself than and explanation to him.

"Yes." Was his only reply as he handed her the water.

She accepted it gratefully and took a big drink. Her eyes had now fully adjusted to the dark. The faint glow of the coals showed her enough of his face to see the hesitation and worry there.

"I'm fine." She said, taking another drink.

"Oh, I'm sure." His voice thick with sarcasm. His mouth tugged up a little on one side. She watched as his ears twitched in their nervous hypervigilant tick she had now come to recognize.

Arida felt a shiver run through her. Being in the shadow of the mountains had caused the air to have a chill to it even in the day. With it now dark, and their fire gone Arida's sweat slick skin quickly cooled. Her clothes now sticking tight to her, drawing out all her body heat.

Noticing her shiver, Faelyn quickly went to work, stoking the coals. Slowly bringing them back to life. Small flames licked at the stick he used to stir them. He laid new branches across it, allowing one to catch fire before laying another.

Once he got the fire back to a suitable size Faelyn grabbed Arida's cloak that she had thrown aside during her nightmare and brought it back to her. Wrapping it around her shoulders he sat down close to her, allowing his one arm to press against hers, adding his own body heat to help warm her. At the brush of his arm a cool breeze rushed down her back, calming the angry wounds she could feel were slowly bleeding again.

"Did you want to talk about it?" He asked quietly, looking not at her but at the fire.

She followed his gaze and watched the flames slowly work on devouring the fresh branches.

"You already know what it was about." She replied. She felt his gaze slide to her face but she refused to meet it. Eventually he too went back to watching the fire. If her silence bothered him, he didn't say. The bleeding once again stopped and she began to warm up thanks to the cloak and fire.

Arida's head slowly drooped until Faelyn gently helped her lay back down , sleep finding her again quickly. He had then walked the perimeter of the small camp site. Looking for any signs of danger or if they were being watched.

Arida had luckily not screamed out during her nightmare, and the light that came from the relic around her neck had been mostly contained to their small shelter. But even so, his guard training made it so he could not find rest until he was sure they were safe.

When he was finally satisfied no one was close, he pulled his bed closer to Arida before laying down next to the princess and quickly found sleep. The day of tending to her and then his trek to town had exhausted his body more than he had let on.

Chapter Thirty Three

Only when the sun rose above the trees enough to enter the cover of the rock did the pair finally stir.

Arida sat up gently, her muscles still sore and strained. The scabs on her back pulled her skin tight. But she felt stronger, like she could move again without breaking her injuries open. She slowly moved her knees, pulling them nearly to her chest before gently leaning forward attempting to stand. As she did, Faelyn was suddenly awake and before her with a hand reached out to help and the other braced to catch should her legs give out. She gave him a small smile before accepting the helping hand to rise.

Her leg muscles groaned in protest, and for a split second she thought they would be uncooperative as they wobbled slightly. But they held and as she straightened her back, she felt the world whirl around her for a moment as she reoriented herself. She was relieved when it steadied. She gripped Faelyn's hand tight as she hesitantly took a step. His muscles flexed as he braced to take on her weight should she fail. But her feet shifted and her legs held. They both seemed to let out a sigh of relief.

"I think we can get moving again today." She said looking up from her feet to Faelyn's face. She saw the hesitation there. "Slowly, but we do need to get moving. We've spent enough time here. It's only a matter of time before Gallis sends men out here looking for me. He has probably already arrived to the cave and discovered me gone and his men dead." The elf's eyes darkened slightly as he remembered killing the afore mentioned men.

"Your right. We will travel on foot, there is no point in getting horses when you still can't ride. Besides, it's easier to traverse the mountains that way. Especially if we get cornered."

"Do you still think we can find a ship that will take us?" Arida asked watching Faelyn's face closely.

His eyes met hers. "I'm not sure. By now Gallis could have gotten word out to all the harbors and ports in Aiden. Us being in Moon's Bay probably tipped him off to our idea. I'm sure for a price we can hire passage. But at that point, I fear loyalties have already been bought and we would find ourselves empty handed and delivered right to your uncle."

Their faces went grim at the idea.

"I did have an idea though..." Faelyn said, his gaze fierce yet worried.

"And that is?" Arida asked, a little hesitant. She also just realized she was still tightly gripping his hand. She relaxed it a little, the movement seeming to remind him of their touch as well. He released her hand at once, her skin prickled at the sudden loss of heat from his skin.

"You said your mother had told you history of the amulet you wear, but did she ever tell you why it reacts with your emotions so strongly?"

"No, I feel she was going to after what had happened in the throne room. But she was never given the chance. What does that have to do with us now though?"

"I was thinking, I might know someone who would know more about it. Someone who may have answers to why it acts the way it does, and why it's so important to your family, besides being an heirloom."

Arida looked at Faelyn, and then glanced away. Her gaze sweeping through the nearby trees. The motion of looking for eavesdroppers had become habit. Her mother had taught her so many things about court, and etiquette, her family history, but only to a certain extent. The lessons would always end just shy of the true purpose of it all, her mother telling her the rest she would learn when she was older. Then, she would change the subject into history of nearby kingdoms and territories. And Arida had patiently accepted this. Always knowing that she would learn the truth eventually. It had never crossed her mind that events could happen and they would cut off her lessons before she learned anything that truly mattered. She hadn't told

Faelyn fully about how the amulet sensed and alerted to the magic of spellborns. But she did want to know as well why it had been reacting to her so much. After it's show last night was triggered by a threat made up in her mind Arida had a small feeling of fear directed towards it now. It would be nice to get some answers about the item she guarded so close and had tied so tightly to her life.

"We are going to have to cross through the mountains to get there though."

Arida racked her memories trying to think of the map of Aiden in her head for what laid on the other side of the Mathwich Mountains. There was a small costal village, a lot of forests, and then...

"You want to go to the North Forest." She all but whispered. Faelyn's grim expression was all the answer she needed.

"And why do you think they would know anything?" She asked, studying his features. The ones she had grown so used to that they were no longer blaringly obvious to her as signs that he was in fact different from her.

The pointed ears, the smooth skin and slightly tilted eyes. The grace and speed with which he moved that at first seemed so fast and unnatural but was now perfectly normal to her. She studied these features now, and his eyes met hers with a look that showed he too was seeing them.

"I grew up there. The elders, they had stories about the dark times. About the magic that used to be here and that is no longer. I think you can feel it, that somehow that piece around your neck holds traces of that magic. And after the orders his men were working off of it's clear the amulet was what he really wanted, not you. Don't you think we should know why he is willing to collapse the entire kingdom to get it?"

"And do you believe it would be safe there?" Arida asked. It was never a secret that the elves loved magic and the power it gave them. History itself had shown that they grew drunk on that power and would go to great lengths to get it back. The one thing Arida would not do was become the one that handed this most protected object over to power hungry creatures after generations of her family keeping it safe.

"I believe I can keep you safe." He said. "Hiding you away is no longer a viable option. And unless you have another idea, I think this is the best plan we've got. It's only a matter of time before we are caught up to again. I don't know about you, but I would rather be in the one place in this world Gallis and his men will not follow us into. "

He was right, they didn't really have any other option. They couldn't very well keep wandering the countryside hoping to find a suitable exit to another country, and even if they had found a boat that would take them across the sea, it's not as if they would find asylum. She was an unannounced, not to mention uninvited royal.

With a deep sigh Arida relented "Okay, we will go to the North Forest and speak to the elders. But we need to be discreet. They must not be made aware that it is I who carry the amulet. We make it seem that my mother has it in her care. Hidden in the castle, and she has sent us on a mission to discover how it can help us. While there I can hide it from view." She reached up and gently brushed the chain.

Faelyn nodded. "The trek there won't be easy. We will have to climb higher and cut through the Twins. It may be autumn here, but up there it is always winter. And magic used to run through these mountains very strongly, and it left its effects behind."

"Like outside of Moon's Bay?" Arida asked remembering the strange plants outside the wall.

"Yes, there will be parts similar to what we saw. But out here, it affected the creatures as well. Animals that were once ordinary that due to magical influences have evolved in ways we never thought would happen. It is a large regret of my people that this happened, elves have always loved and valued the land and the part we played in altering it in such ways has weighed heavily on our hearts."

Faelyn's tone was low and sad. Arida could tell that though he had not been alive when his people acted in the ways they had, he to took responsibility for it.

"Do you know the way?" Is all she asked, hoping that a slight change in subject would ease his thoughts.

"Yes, I have traveled this way before. During short leaves I used to get I would take the opportunity to go back home. Especially if those breaks fell on a holiday or celebration. Even with your injuries it should not take us long to get there. A couple of days perhaps to get to the beginning of the passage. And then from there just another few to hit the boundary of the forest. I don't think we need to try to rush. Even with Gallis's men following they will hesitate to follow deep into the mountains."

Faelyn reached down and grabbed the cloak she had dropped while standing and fastened it around her shoulders.

"Then I guess we should get packed up and get moving."

Chapter Thirty Four

Faelyn had insisted on packing up their camp entirely by himself. Unwilling to allow her to even tie their pack strings closed. Though after he had to help her put on and then lace up her boots, she didn't have a lot of ammunition to argue with. He did though concede on letting her carry one of the packs after she insisted, but only after he transferred ninety percent of its contents into his own.

The pack, though quite a bit smaller than her previous one and mostly empty was still heavy enough on her weakened muscles that Arida knew they would not be able to travel far or fast today. The thickness of her shirt and cloak helped cushion it from rubbing on her torn skin.

Faelyn watched her closely the first few minutes of their walk, keeping in stride beside her. But once he had decided she was not going to collapse into the dirt he took a slight lead ahead navigating them through the forest.

They had not traveled far into the mountains to get to their small cave. As soon as they ventured out, Arida looked around and saw they were in more of a valley between some of the smaller foothills. The larger peaks were just before them, towering and ominous. The tops of which were snowcapped and foggy.

"Don't worry." Faelyn said following her gaze up. "We won't be cresting those anytime soon. Our path will keep us lower down."

A small shiver raked through Arida and she rolled her shoulders in a stretching way to try to hide her nerves. Her skin tugged and pulled in different directions, reminding her not to do that anymore.

The walk out of their valley proved fairly easy. The ground was soft and gave Arida's feet plenty of grip. She was once again glad she didn't have to break in new boots again. The tree canopy created a nice blockage from the bright afternoon sun which the small party was glad for since they had donned their winter cloaks to keep their packs lighter. Arida could see the sheen of sweat on Faelyn's forehead and could feel it mirrored on her own, though the air was getting more of a bite to it the exertion of the hike kept them both warm.

Faelyn would pause from time to time, looking around like he was examining some animal trail or sign. But she always knew those breaks were for her. Allowing her a moment to lean a shoulder against a tree and relieve the pressure from her back while he stayed silently nearby.

But Arida didn't mind the walking, even if it caused her discomfort with every step. The walking helped keep her mind from wandering. Instead of thinking about the men from the cave she focused on the loose rocks and crawling roots underfoot. Instead of hearing the crack of the whip or smell the burning of her flesh, she would listen for water or the rustle of the wind through the branches.

They made good distance despite their slow pace. It wasn't long before the ground began to slowly incline, the terrain turning rocky. The trees growing only lower off the edges of the small ridges forming. They tried to stay as close to the trees as they could, avoiding the large openings where they could be easily spotted from those further down.

Just as they were leaving the small foothills and reaching their first true inclined mountain side Faelyn stopped. "I think we should rest here for the night. We have good cover here, and it will be growing dark soon."

Arida looked up at the sky, the sun had still not sunk below the tree line. Reading her skepticism, he added.

"It gets darker faster here now that we have gained elevation. As soon as the sun goes behind those trees, it will go from day to instant night. I want to have time to make a proper camp and get a fire going before then. We are warm now from walking but it will grow cold once the sun is gone."

Arida needed no further persuading, she said nothing but slowly moved to the small tree cover beside them and dropped her pack. She ground her teeth to keep the moan from escaping her lips as she straightened her spine. Her back felt rubbed raw, but there didn't appear to be any fresh blood. Which puzzled her, as bad as her wounds were yesterday, they should not be as advanced in their healing as they were acting. The bruises on her wrists from the shackles were already fading to a yellowish green on the edges. She fiddled with the chain around her neck wondering if the amulet had something to do with it. If it was somehow healing her? Maybe this was one of the ways it protected the royal family as it was fabled to do.

She noticed Faelyn watching her closely from where he had dropped his own pack. She quickly released the chain and let it fall back under the cover of her neckline and busied herself with finding sticks and branches from around them and using her foot scooched them over to what would be the center of the camp.

Again, he stayed silent, letting her be while he pulled the bedrolls out and positioned them around where she had left the sticks. He then moved to the pack she had been carrying and pulled two blankets out, laying one with each bedroll.

Within moments the fire was also started and their camp was set. Faelyn had been right, the sun was almost below the tops of the trees, casting a warm glow through the pine branches. Shadows already formed close to their bases. The birds had quieted, a few soaring back their nests for the night.

Faelyn used the last bit of light to walk a perimeter around them, making sure there were no prying eyes, or predators nearby that may disturb them.

Arida used the few moments alone to relieve herself behind the trees. During her bathroom trip she had finally had a chance to see the injuries to her legs and abdomen. She had been to chicken to look earlier. Afraid the shock of seeing her damaged skin would prevent her from making the trek. Though her torso and upper legs had not been used as savagely as her back had, she was still shocked to see that her burns which were only days old appeared to be several weeks into healing. It couldn't possibly be the salve Faelyn had used. There was no way something from Clarea had anything in it advanced enough for this kind if healing. When she returned to camp and Faelyn was still not back yet. She slowly lifted the edge of her shirt. Sliding her hands under the material she felt up the skin on her back. Careful not to scratch any of the markings with her fingernails.

The skin was rough, thick veins of damaged skin wound in odd shapes. Following the path, the whip had taken. Smooth skin broke them up into a strange pattern. The wounds themselves felt like bands of cord had been sewn under her skin. The muscles bunched and tight. She could feel the roughness of scabbing in some places. But was shocked there were not more. The majority of them were just odd semi healed skin.

Arida paused for a moment. Her mind trying to figure out how she had become this far along in healing. There was though, a small vain part of her that worried if her back would stay this bumpy, corded mess, forever marked by that night?

She didn't hear Faelyn coming up behind her. His steps too soft and quiet even on the rocky ground. His fingers met hers and he slowly pulled them away from their examination. He made no comment of the accelerated healing. She looked up at his face. His expression gave nothing away as his eyes met hers. She stared into them, momentarily lost in the green depths. Had she never noticed before how the green got darker close to the iris. He stared back too, seeming to have similar thoughts going through his mind. He glanced quicky down to where their hands mingled together against her back and slowly pulled his away.

She too moved her hand, though quicker than he had, letting her top shift back into place.

"I found some berries and edible roots while I was checking around. We can eat it tonight with some of the dried meat I got from the village. Hopefully once we get further in and are less likely to be followed, I can spare some time to try to hunt for small game. Preserve our dried food stash for when we are higher up and all life becomes scarce."

Arida responded with a short nod and went to sit on her bed roll. She accepted her share of the berries and quickly popped some in her mouth. The dark fruit was tart and reminded her of a medicine her nurse maid used to make her drink when she felt poorly. But she ate them without complaint.

They once again ate with only the sounds of the fire and nature surrounding them. Faelyn had been right to start the fire when he had. Arida could feel the temperature slowly cool as they sat there. She huddled closer to the flames, letting the warmth fight off the chill.

"Will it always be like this?" She asked finally breaking the silence. She looked up at the elf sitting across from her. He watched the flames dance; he didn't have to ask what she meant before he looked up and answered.

"I don't know what your future holds. If you will be forced to always travel from one town to the next. If you will ever get to settle. I am hoping we find answers to that question when we get to the North Forest."

He looked back down and Arida contemplated his words. 'Your future' he had said not 'our future'. Was he planning his trip to end when he got to the North Forest? It was after all, his home. He would be safe there, and could live out the rest of his life in the forest. Even if marked as a traitor to Aiden, the elves wouldn't turn him over to Gallis. But that same loyalty didn't extend to her, she was sure.

What would she do if he left? The thought had never occurred to her. He had made her mother a promise, to keep her safe. Had she been selfish in thinking that it meant even if she had to leave this country forever that he would accompany her? That he too would leave behind everything he had known, for her? All for a princess he had hardly known a few months and rarely spoke to him unless it was about her plans for her own safety.

Arida sat there lost in her thoughts until even the sun had gone for the night. And when it was just the soft flames flicking light and shadows across her face as she stared into it, she didn't even notice the small glimpses the man sitting across from her made, going quietly mad at the silent thoughts he saw race through her mind in the tiny changes of her face he had studied and memorized in the months he had spent with her. And how he wondered what he would read on that face when she learned his secret.

Chapter Thirty Five

The night had been colder than any of the others Arida had experienced since her travels had begun. She woke several times in the night, burrowed under her blanket and in a tight stiff ball as close to the fire as she dared get. During one of the times the cold had roused her she could have sworn she had caught sight of eyes flashing in the shrubs that laid behind the outline of Faelyn's body. But the impossible height of them and therefore the beast's height had confused her tired brain back into sleep. Faelyn had told her the remnants of magic that had been left had not only caused odd changes to the plant life but also to the animals that had inhabited the area as well. Arida just had yet to witness for herself what those changes looked like.

Just as dawn started to peak its way through the trees Arida woke again and glanced toward her companion who was already up and adding wood to the fire. Stiff and sore Arida stretched her limbs in hopes of loosening the tightness but also to warm up a bit before they continued their long hike.

"We had some visitors last night." She said in hopes he had noticed the eyes as well and she wasn't going crazy.

"Yeah, I think you'd classify it as a bear if you really had to." He poked at the fire stirring the coals to catch the new pieces.

Arida shivered and scooted closer to the fire. She recalled the look of the bear that was stuffed and sitting in her father's study back home, a relic from a previous king's proud hunt. The creature had been a formidable size to be sure. But compared to the height of the eyes last night it had to have been at least double the size of the one in the study.

"It was just curious." Faelyn said and looked up at her, humor evident on his face. "Harmless really... except for the razor claws and teeth capable of tearing into you as easily as you tore into that rabbit."

Arida gave him a hand gesture she had seen a few times from men in the castle when they hadn't realized she was present. This only caused a loud laugh from him in response as he stacked another piece of wood on the fire. The sound echoed off the trees, a chorus of excited bird chirps followed. The forest itself seemed to respond to the sound of his laughter and that thought settled Arida's nerves just a little bit that evening.

They delayed hiking out that morning until the sun had poked out from behind the mountain enough to make it somewhat bearable to leave the fire. They hiked for hours with the only change being their altitude and the weather that came along with it. The higher they hiked the colder it became. And so their routine went for the next few days. Hike, camp, freeze, repeat.

Finally, one night when they discovered frost growing across their camp in the shadows the sun left as it sank behind the trees Faelyn unpacked his bed roll and laid it beside Arida's. She didn't say any-thing when he did but he must have still felt the need to explain.

"There's no point in freezing to death out here. We will be much warmer at night if we share body heat.

She again made no response, just pulled out a few of the precious strips of dried meat they had left and handed some to him with a small smile. He returned it and tore into the stiff jerky.

They had crossed a few different game trails during the days, but according to Faelyn nothing fresh enough to hunt off of. They had run out of fruit to scavenge the day the frost stayed even when the sun was out. Arida had recognized a small twiggy plant from one of her studies that was used to make teas. It had been weak and bitter when they boiled it with stream water. But it had been hot and it filled their stomachs enough to ebb the hunger during their afternoon meal times.

Arida's body grew stronger as well. Her legs no longer felt as if they threatened to give out at the slightest twinge. Her back didn't ache or reopen the wounds anymore. She again was surprised by how quickly the lash marks and burns had healed. They were still sore and had small scabs in the places she took the most hits. But on the edges of her back, where just the tip of the whip had grazed once or twice the marks had turned into angry red bunches of scar tissue. The bruises on her wrists were now just a faint dull mark that barely even hurt when she pressed gingerly against them.

On the one-week mark of their trek they did in fact hit their goal. Arida would have known she had hit the milestone even if she had not been traveling with an elf. A path appeared in the middle of the forest, seemingly out of nowhere.

It wasn't wide, only big enough for two people to walk side by side. It wasn't paved, or even worn away to dirt. But in fact, was more of a long section where only grass grew. The underbrush, shrubs and various other plants they had been whacking and trudging through seemed to end at the same point along the border. A twisted tree grew on either side of the entrance, reaching up and curving over the path, creating a natural arch.

The frost was thicker here too. Almost crunching like ice. It gave the grass path an ominous grey tone. Arida shivered, but from the cold or the feeling this obviously magic made structure gave her she wasn't sure.

"We will follow this path the rest of the way." Faelyn said with a slight frown.

"What's the problem?" Arida asked looking around for anything she may have missed.

"I haven't worried about our path or trail because of all the brush it was easy for me to hide our footprints or other markings as animal caused. But with the frost being so thick now on the trail I worry that if someone has been following us, or even just looking for us up here, they will be easily led right to us."

"Can we just walk beside the trail? Close enough to see when it bends or changes but far enough away to keep us from being spotted?" Arida asked not understanding why they had to walk directly on the path.

"No, the path is only visible at its start. It was built centuries ago on almost a fault line of sorts for magic. And it's one of the few spells that has remained intact after all these decades. If one were to walk across it without first walking through the arch it would not appear to you as a path at all. You would just think you happened across a small patch of low growing brush and continue on your way. There is an ancient spelled locked into those trees that allows one to see the path as they are on it. And as long as one of us remains on it the other should be able to exit and refind it, objects on the path aren't hidden. So, we will have to be cautious. But this passage will take us right to one of the entrances to the North Forest."

Arida knew that long lasting spells and old magic had rules, but she had never known they could be so exact and precise in their functions.

"So, we take the path then?" She asked unsure of what his hesitation was.

"This is the fastest, most direct route. But it leaves us vulnerable, if we are followed there's nowhere to hide on the path. Our other option is to keep hiking through the brush until we reach a border. The elves will know when we are close and will send someone to retrieve us from the border and bring us in. But with that option we risk a... less understanding welcome. Though as the princess, you should be safe."

"Should be?" She turned and stared at him.

He glanced back at her "Some elves might still react, unfavorably to my bringing not only a human into their most private territory, but the rogue princess of Aiden."

It crossed Arida's mind again that the elves may not be so willing to offer her the safety she was looking for. She may be their princess, but she was far from her palace. And it was after all her ancestor who had not only locked down magic, but destroyed the elves strongest ally and moved them from a place of power to a step above servant.

"Don't worry." Faelyn said fully facing her. "No one will attack you when we cross the border. Just as anyone else seeking asylum, we will be brought in front of the governor and questioned. That doesn't mean they will not make it known their dislike for you being there though. My hope is after explaining the situation and what your uncle is doing, the govenor will help us come up with a more permanent solution."

A game of politics. That's what Arida realized she would be entering as soon as she stepped foot across that border. And she had until the end of the path to figure out exactly how she was going to play it.

"Surely, he must know what is happening. Gallis hasn't exactly kept it a secret that he is the one now in charge and searching for me. He had to have sent word to the governor as soon as he realized we were running." Even without magic the elves were a powerful race. That was one of the reasons why the crown had allowed them to retreat into their forest when magic fell. And, for the most part, govern themselves within the confines of their territory. To put too tight of a leash would have pushed them to openly rebel and another dark blight was not what the newly free kingdom needed. And it had stayed as such since.

"One would think if he hadn't sent word himself, an informant of the governor would have heard and told him." Faelyn glanced back at the path. "So which way shall it be?"

Arida looked once towards her companion and then back to the path before her.

She walked slowly, closely examining the twisted tree arch. "I think the path is our best shot. If we are going in to request help, I would like to do so the proper way."

Faelyn nodded then strode forward, through the arch before pausing to turn towards her.

Arida followed, the grass was soft and cushioned beneath her feet, a nice relief from the rocky ground they had been traversing.

"How long does the path go on for?" She asked as a small warmth tickled at her skin as she passed under the arch.

"It goes on for a few miles. We will stop and make camp along the way, but we should reach the entrance by tomorrow."

She walked a few more steps in until she stopped where Faelyn was still paused.

"What is it?" Arida asked quietly looking around for any sign of trouble.

"Nothing's wrong." He assured her. "I've just heard history of humans using the path before the uprising. But it's been close to a century since a human stepped foot on the path. I wasn't entirely sure if it was just from lack of need... or if something else prevented them from entering." He shrugged his shoulders at her gaped expression which she corrected as soon as she caught herself doing it. She couldn't believe it; he had just let her walk through the arch without so much as a warning beforehand that old magic might have done something to keep her out.

"So much for having a guard." She muttered and marched forward, her hands balled into fists at her sides. He chuckled and caught up, retaking the lead.

The amulet was a soft warm comfort to Arida as she followed the elf path past the first curve of trees and closer to the North Forest.

Chapter Thirty Six

C hapter 36

The trees grew taller and closer together the farther they walked. The path kept fairly even though there were the occasional dips and turns, but the ground itself kept smooth under foot. It was a small relief to Arida, her back had begun to ache from the exertion of keeping her balance when rocks and branches would slide out from under her on their earlier rocky trek.

After about a mile or two Faelyn had chosen to stop for the night. If it hadn't been for him telling her the sun was about to go down, she wouldn't have known. The compactness of the trees had made their walk dim from almost the beginning. It could have been noon or dusk for all she could tell. But it also made it the perfect spot to keep concealed while in the path.

"You stay here on the path and start making camp. I'm going to see if I can find us something to eat." He waited for her nod before he took a step off the grass and onto the rock covered dirt that surrounded them. She watched him curiously as he slowly and quietly stalked away in a slightly hunched hunters walk. He turned once and glanced over his shoulder, Arida guessed to check that he could still see her and therefor return to the path when he was ready. His expression stayed cool and neutral and he turned back and disappeared into the dim trees.

Arida worked quietly and quickly unpacking their things from the pack she had removed off her back and Faelyn's that he had left, she hadn't even noticed him take it off before he disappeared into the trees. When Arida pulled the bedrolls out, she struggled for the first time since they had been traveling together. Where should she put them? Across from each other like they used to be? Or side by side the way they had been the last few nights? The feelings these little rolls of fabric were creating in Arida was enough to drive her mad. But even working at a slow pace and rearranging the bed rolls numerous times, she was still finished long before Faelyn came back.

He had a couple of small pieces of raw meat already dressed and ready for cooking. They almost appeared to be chicken breasts so Arida assumed they were wild birds of some kind that he had shot with his sling shot and cleaned far from their camp site. Arida hadn't thought about it before if the charm on the path worked to deter wild animals from those using it. She slowly scanned the now dark tree line.

Within minutes of being back, Faelyn had started the fire, placed the pieces of meat on sticks and began roasting them from his seat on his bed roll across from Arida's, the struggle she had with its placement completely unknown to him.

He stoked the fire; the smell of the cooking meat filled the air. Arida heard the rustle of leaves around them. A large cat like creature prowled from the darkness of the trees. It's nose sniffing in the air, scenting the meat. It was unlike any animal Arida had ever seen. It was far bigger than the forest cats she would see in the books she studied. The fur was thick and grey with a shadow of spots. Its feet though large were silent as it prowled, aside from the occasional rustle of grass and leaves.

She glanced over at Faelyn to see him staring at her. His finger rose to his mouth to signal to her to stay quiet. The beast had yet to see them thanks to them sitting near the brush that bordered the path.

It turned its large head and stared almost through her. Arida's breath caught in her throat at the large green eyes that seemed to glow in the dim firelight.

The animal continued to stalk around trying to find the source of the scent. The pair didn't dare move, even to take the meat off the fire when the outside turned dark and burned. Faelyn kept his gaze trained on the animal, watching it closely.

At the strong smell of the burning meat, the strange mountain cat turned and prowled back into the forest.

Once its shadow disappeared into the night, Arida relaxed.

They did their best to salvage their now sad excuse for a dinner. The meat was tough and chewy. The ends tasted of charcoal and dust. But it was better than an empty belly so Arida chewed without complaint.

More creatures milled about as the evening went on so they kept conversation to a minimum. Arida actually rather enjoyed seeing what animals appeared. Even though many of them looked more than capable of killing them with their claws, teeth and, on some occasions, spikes. Having and elf close by who was used to such creatures helped ease her wariness. He didn't seem frightened or put off by their appearances, so neither was she.

After a small herd of what appeared to be large turkey's that sniffed and growled like some sort of dog Arida broke their silence. "I'm surprised about how many of these animals we are encountering. Is it because we are getting closer to the North Forest?"

Faelyn chuckled. His arms were crossed behind his head, allowing him to angle farther to see her better. "There have always been a lot of animals like these around our camps. Maybe not as active as they have been tonight, but they've been there."

Arida's shock kept her from forming a response.

"The lasting effects of the magic that has altered their appearance has also given many of them a higher intelligence, making them good at hiding and camouflaging when they are around camps, villages and the castle. But I assume that this close to the North Forest allows them to feel safer with their roaming."

Arida had almost wished she had gone with her feeling of putting their sleep rolls closer together.

"We will be alright here as long as we stay quite." Faelyn whispered as he shifted, settling back down to sleep. She heard him murmur something else, something strange and spoken in a whisper under his breath. But her eyes had grown heavy and soon sleep pulled her under and her mind drifted and dreamed of green eyes.

Chapter Thirty Seven

C hapter 37A large thud, the rustle of leaves, and a hand yanking her arm is what woke Arida.

The sky was still dark, their fire dim when Arida was roughly pulled to her feet. Faelyn was crouched across the fire staring at her. The tip of a sword rested under his chin. His red hair glowed in the small licks of flames that still worked at the logs. Arida followed the sword up the blade to the hilt where it was joined by a hand and then the arm of a soldier that stared down at the elf who knelt before him.

She glanced to her left at the man who held her arm in a vise grip that was beginning to prevent blood flow.

Another soldier stood behind the two that held them captive.

"We had a feeling you would be coming this way, trying to find help from the other filth of your kind." The one holding the sword to Faelyn's throat said, tilting the tip up and hitting his chin.

"It was only too simple to find the start of the path, with some help." The soldier with the sword glanced up to the one holding Arida's arm.

She followed his glance and through the slight flicker of light from the flames Arida could see the tips of pointed ears... an elf. A knot filled her stomach. If this elf had already switched sides to help Gallis, then why wouldn't all of them? Faelyn could be the odd one out. One of the few that didn't wish to see the darkness of magic come back. If the rest though had all decided to back Gallis, then she was without hope.

As if he could see the despair whirling inside her, Faelyn locked his gaze on Arida. Ignoring the sword at his throat he whispered.

"Not all of us are traitorous filth that wish to see the kingdom pulled apart and ruled by a madman."

The hand on Arida's arm squeezed harder, deadening it further. Her abused muscles protested, reawakening the pain from the hours the arms spent hung in suspension. Arida gritted her teeth to keep from making a sound.

Arida curled her fingers into tight fists. Fighting the feeling and willing the limb not to go numb.

"What took you weeks to run from on foot will take us just a few days ride to drag you back. Your uncle wants to see you very badly. He has great plans for you and that fancy trinket you have around your neck. Since you seem to like it so much perhaps he will make it your collar." The one with the sword and apparently the only voice out of the trio said with sneer.

"And a very pretty collar it will be." The soldier off to the side laughed.

This roused a feeling in Arida that she had worked for years to keep in check. An inner rage that like a wild fire consumed everything in its path as fast as it could from the point of ignition until someone put it out. It was something she had fought with since she was a small child. It was a huge part of the reason she had begun her lessons as young as she did. To learn not to lash out to those who stoked her anger, especially when it didn't take much.

The side effect of fighting with her anger was the very reason she was so stoic with every emotion. To unleash one, was to unleash all. And once unleashed Arida's anger would overwhelm her, and she could feel it now. Burning at the edges of her mind, begging to be unleashed. Her cheeks grew warm as she fought it. It had been so long since she had truly gotten angry, learning to ignore things and move on rather than to acknowledge any feeling at all. And she wasn't sure why this was finally the moment. Maybe after going so far and through so much. A familiar warmth started growing at her chest,

"And what do we do with the elf?" The man behind them asked, looking at Faelyn as if he already had an idea of what he wanted to do to him. And when his gaze flickered to the elf holding Arida she could see he was holding the same option open to all elvish kind, even ones on his own side

"Our orders were to only bring the princess back alive and unharmed; nothing was said about her little travel companion." The sword pushed slightly into Faelyn's throat drawing a small bead of blood.

And as that bead began a slow roll down his throat, highlighted by a slightly brighter than it had been fire Arida could feel her whole face flush. Her fist curled tighter until her palms stung from the nails biting into them.

"You. Will. Not. Touch. Him." Arida heard her voice cold and strong say.

The guard with the sword slowly turned his head to look at her. "Oh, I won't? Well, what if I cut off his head and let you carry it all the way back to the castle. Will that make you feel better?"

The man grinned and the flames in the fire had grown so large now Arida could see he was missing most of his teeth. The fire was hot and its flames danced, licking the edge of the rocks containing it. The men seemed to notice it now. Even Faelyn's expression widened slightly at the flames that moved unprovoked as if living.

"What the..." Was all the elf holding Arida got out before she took her free right fist and with all her might thrust it up right into his nose. The heat at her chest was now searing, and Arida used the pain to feed into her rage.

She heard a satisfying crunch and the elf started swearing. Before he could blink Arida was on the man with the sword, clawing at his face and she realized she was screaming as she scratched skin away from his face and pulled her nails down his eyes.

All Arida could see was red as she felt the man let go of the sword to try to push her away from him. As soon as his grip relaxed Faelyn grabbed hold of the sword and in one standing movement gutted the third man who lingered behind watching Arida's fit of rage.

The man she was clawing was unsuccessful in his attempt to pry her from him and instead began walking backwards trying to use his hands to block hers. He stumbled over a rock and she used his momentum to take him to the ground. Her claws turned back into fists and she was hitting him over and over again striking him in the nose, the eyes, anywhere she could make contact. The small bead of blood running down Faelyn's neck all she could see.

She pulled her arm back again and it was caught in a strong hand. She whirled, expecting to see one elf and instead saw hers. His green eyes were the only thing that broke through the shade of red that had covered her vision.

"I've got you." Was all he said to her, his voice calm and steady. And in that moment, it was all she needed to hear. In a rush of emotion still running through her Arida couldn't stop herself as she threw her mouth against his. His hand still enveloped her fist as she formed her lips against his. Arida found herself moving her body to meld against his, leaning against him to better angle the kiss. His chest was hard and strong against hers. His free hand grabbed her lower back in response, pulling her even closer. He released her fist and caressed her arm all the way down until he stilled it at the base of her neck. His mouth responded swiftly, pushing against hers, moving with her, he tasted of rain water and forest berries. The heat burning at Arida's chest now seemed to come from deep insider her rather than from the necklace.

Abruptly Faelyn broke the kiss. Arida opened her eyes to see his still inches from her face. They had a heat in them she had not seen before. A heat that she felt was mirrored in her own expression. Men had never been something Arida had thought of much. She was always kept too busy to socialize with more than the obnoxious dukes and earls-to-be she had grown up with. And even the ones who had visited from other countries in hopes of negotiating a treaty for her hand hadn't even come close to looking like Faelyn. Or making her feel the way she did with him.

Her heart still beat strongly against her chest.

"We need to get moving, the animals will smell the blood soon and be on this spot quickly."

Arida felt her emotions getting back under her control as she looked around at the carnage they had created.

The man Faelyn had stabbed in the belly had died quickly, as had the elf who had held her. His throat was sliced but the hand that had held her was also severed completely from his body, as if suffering its own death from assaulting her.

The man Arida had gotten to had not faired so cleanly. His face was a bloody unrecognizable mash of broken and bruised skin. She had actually clawed one eye almost out of the socket.

Arida didn't remember every move she had made; in fact, she didn't remember a whole lot of the attack itself now that it was over and the haze that had fallen over her had faded. But staring at the carnage of the man she had beaten to death made a sickening feeling rose in her throat.

"You had no choice." Faelyn said, his hand still on her lower back.

"I know." Was the only response Arida could get out as she looked down at her hands, the knuckles were red and swollen, the bruises already forming.

Faelyn looked down at them as well as she stroked a thumb over a spot that was already forming a large angry dark bruise. Arida worried the knuckle might be broken. He released her back and reached for the hand, gently he followed the same movement she had done. Brushing his thumb over the spot. The skin tingled and she looked at him, trying to catch his gaze. He just slowly lowered her hand and looked around them.

"We need to get going."

Arida kept her gaze on him as he turned from her and started kicking dirt over the back to small fire.

Just as the final flame sizzled out Faelyn whipped his head around, his worried expression made Arida follow his gaze and looked back down the path from the direction they had come. But all she saw was darkness tinged with the slight beginning of morning light.

"We have to run." Was all Faelyn said before he grabbed her hand again, this time with urgency and began running once again. Abandoning all of their belongings they didn't already have strapped to their bodies.

Arida was pulled along at first until she was able to get her legs up to his speed. She felt the muscles in her back burn as she exerted herself.

"What... is... it." She managed to gasp, trying to catch a look over her shoulder to see what he had.

"More soldiers were with them, waiting for them to bring us out. When they didn't arrive, they grew concerned. They were walking slowly and carefully, but once they find their friends, they will be on us quickly so we have to keep going." He tugged her hand again as if to exaggerate what he had just said. Her hand stung from his tight grip. But not as badly as she had thought it should.

Her mind traveled back as they ran, as if the exercise made the memory clearer. The tingling she had felt when he examined her hand, she had felt it before, with her back. She had felt it when she had woken up after her rescue, and again whenever he would examine it and apply his salve.

She also thought back to last night, his quiet murmuring before bed, and afterwards she hadn't heard another animal around them all night.

She couldn't help it; her feet came to a stop at once. Her hand ripped from Faelyn's as he kept running. He looked back in surprise.

"What are you doing? They are right behind us!" He quietly yelled.

"You healed me, didn't you?" She asked staring at him, not breaking eye contact as his grew ever so slightly wider. "You healed me... with magic. You're Spellborn?"

"Yes." Was his only reply.

Arida sucked in her next breath and held it. Unable to let it out, unable to accept the truth he had just blandly stated. Her advanced healing after he had rescued her from the cave, that had been him. And the shadows she had seen under his eyes when she had woken, were those the result of the magic use? And had that been what had caused the tingling? Not some healing balm he had picked up. This triggered another memory, one of the same tingling feeling after he had discovered her on the bathroom floor. All of the signs had been there, how had she had not figured it out?

Most importantly why hadn't the amulet? According to her mother it was supposed to signal to her when a Spellborn was performing magic nearby. Or had it?

She suddenly remembered the slight warming sensation that accompanied those moments. She had always associated it with the attacks, or the magic pockets in the land they came across. Never him.

"Why didn't you tell me?" She finally asked after a heartbeat of silence.

"I don't think this is the best place to discuss this. I promise you when we get to safety, I will explain it. But right now, we need to keep moving. We are close to the border, once we cross it, we will be safe."

"You mean the elves will protect us? Last time I checked the last elf I met tried to kidnap me and one I have been trusting for weeks I just found out has been lying to me the entire time."

Hurt flashed across Faelyn's face, but it was gone in an instant.

"I promise." Was all he said and offered his hand to her.

She looked at it, hesitating to take it and follow someone who had lied to her for this long. What else had he lied about? Were the elves really going to protect her? Or just him?

Twigs snapped behind them and before she could react Faelyn grabbed her hand anyway and swept her into his arms. She sat cradled against his chest as he took off at full speed.

Though impeded by carrying her full weight he still moved faster than when she was running beside him.

Arida threw her arms around his neck to hold on as he sped through the forest. Trees were just dark green blurs as they moved.

Just as Arida thought they had probably lost the soldiers an arrow whizzed by her head, missing her by an inch.

She looked over Faelyn's shoulder and saw two elves garbed in Gallis's colors running behind them. But unlike Faelyn they were not weighed down carrying another person.

They were quickly gaining distance on them. And Arida had a horrible thought. They were running right into Elf territory and they were being chased by elves. Who had just as much right to enter as Faelyn did.

Arida looked straight ahead and noticed what appeared to be an arch, similar to the one that was at the beginning of the path. It was made out of living trees that had curved and twisted around each other creating a similar structure.

"Trust me." Faelyn whispered into Arida's hair.

She looked up and one minute she was gazing into the dark green eyes of the man who set every emotion in her erupting into a confusing puzzle. And the next she was airborne...again.

Chapter Thirty Eight

e'd thrown her. He had actually thrown her. Again!

Air ripped at her hair and tore it loose from the tie that had it secured. She passed through the arch and Arida half expected something to happen when she did. She wasn't entirely sure what, but something to signify her passing into the territory of the elves. But nothing changed.

Except as soon as she passed through the arch, she started losing altitude. The ground came up at her fast and she curled in, bracing herself for impact.

Her shoulder hit first, and then her head followed. It struck the cold hard winter earth with a crack and the world spun. She looked back and could see Faelyn standing just on the other side of the arch. The sword from his back was now held with both his hands, ready to take on the two soldiers running full speed at him. Just before they reached him, though a foot stepped in front of Arida's face blocking her view.

She looked up, the man the foot belonged to tilting as she did.

"Well, well, well. If it isn't the rogue princess of Aiden. Did you know the entire kingdom has been looking for you?"

The elf that stood before her had an ancient air about him. He looked visually the same age as Faelyn, but he exuded an energy, a power that came from someone who had lived a long time and experienced many things. He crouched down and she tried to focus on him as best as she could but the hit to her head was making it difficult.

"And what are we going to do with you?" He asked just as the ringing clash of fighting steal rang out and Arida's vison went black.

About the author

Taylor Rogers grew up in the PNW and found her love of writing in early elementary school, entering writing contests and continuing her love of writing small stories. As an adult Taylor entered into the world of publishing with her debut novel "Out of the Woods" in 2023. Now she starts another first with her breakout into the fantasy genre with her fist book of the Series Spellborn.

Amy Smull Photogra-
phy